SEALS

"You stop now!" came the voice.

But Tynan didn't stop. He reached around and slipped the pistol from his waistband and carefully transferred it to his front pocket. With his thumb, he removed the safety.

The voice came again, but this time it was much closer. The men had started to run, moving quietly along the side of the road. Without a warning, Tynan spun to face them. They stopped suddenly, four abreast. Tynan could see that two of the men were grinning.

"Hey, gringo!" said one of the grinning men. "I think maybe you are CIA. I think maybe you are not going to leave this place in one piece. I think maybe we cut you up for a lesson . . ."

SEALS #3
RESCUE!

STEVE MACKENZIE

AVON
PUBLISHERS OF BARD, CAMELOT, DISCUS AND FLARE BOOKS

SEALS #3: RESCUE! is an original publication of Avon Books. This work has never before appeared in book form. This work is a novel. Any similarity to actual persons or events is purely coincidental.

AVON BOOKS
A division of
The Hearst Corporation
105 Madison Avenue
New York, New York 10016

First Avon Printing: September 1987

AVON TRADEMARK REG. U.S. PAT. OFF. AND IN OTHER COUNTRIES, MARCA REGISTRADA, HECHO EN U.S.A.

Printed in the U.S.A.

K-R 10 9 8 7 6 5 4 3 2 1

1

The black Cadillac limousine with tinted glass and a classic moonroof slid to a halt near the stone pillars and the rusting, wrought-iron gate. Sitting in the front seat were two burly men, both with long dark hair, deep brown eyes, and mustaches. One of them looked exactly like Zapata. In the jump seats were two more men. Each of them wore a navy blue suit, a snowy white shirt, and a striped tie, and each of them had on sunglasses.

Up the winding road behind the massive gate, hidden behind exotic tropical plants loaded with brightly colored flowers and huge green leaves, was a stone building created from the local rock. It housed one of the most exclusive colleges in all of South America. Only the children of the very richest and most powerful families could attend.

Juana Gutierrez, the nineteen-year-old daughter of the new head of the recently formed government of a South American country, had been waiting for the arrival of the limousine. Since her father had taken power in a bloodless coup engineered with the help of several military officers who happened to command key units of the presidental bodyguard, she had been carefully watched because there were now terrorists who would see the value in kidnapping her.

Juana stood on the manicured lawn that climbed the slope from the street and the tropical gardens to the brown stone structure. Overhead the sun blazed in a cloudless sky of a blue so deep and perfect that photographers came from around the world to use it as a backdrop. She watched three younger girls chase one another across the deep green grass, toward the white gazebo that housed a table piled high with food. She heard the horn of the limousine blast once, signaling her that it was time to leave for the day.

Without a word, she picked up the books that were sitting on a stone wall reminiscent of the Incan architecture that dominated much of her homeland, and she trotted down the curving stone driveway. In front of her she saw the limo, its green and white pennant flapping in the late afternoon breeze.

As she approached the gate, a guard, protected by a tiny structure of wood and glass hidden among the landscaped bushes and trees, appeared. He used an huge old key to unlock the gate and swing it open for her. She waved at him as she passed. He was an old man, having served for thirty years on the local police force, and although he wore a gigantic pistol on his hip, no one believed that he had the strength to draw it, let alone fire it.

The taller of the two men, named Luis, got out of the back of the car, holding the rear door open for her. He watched her as she came closer, smiling at her as if he was glad to see her. He touched his forehead almost in a salute and then bowed slightly gesturing at the open door as if to speed her into the limo.

At that moment there was the sound of squealing tires. A beat-up Chevy that once had been blue but was now covered with large red areas of rusting base metal shot around the corner fifty yards away, its tires smoking. The engine raced, backfired, and a cloud of blue exploded from the rear. There was another protest from the tires and the car slid to a halt only inches from the right side of the limousine, its front end nearly touching one of the black doors.

Luis clawed for the weapon he wore concealed beneath his dark suit coat. He dodged to the right as he tried to draw, watching the occupants of the car and trying to knock Juana to the ground to protect her.

The doors of the ambush vehicle flew open, and three men dressed in ragged old clothes, jeans, and ski masks leaped out. One of them opened fire with an AK-47, the rounds catching Luis in the chest and stomach. He was thrown backward, the pistol that he held tossed over his shoulder to clatter to the street. He fell to the ground and rolled over once, his blood staining his white shirt crimson.

One of the other gunmen began to hose down the limousine, firing at the windows, but the slugs bounced and ricocheted off the bulletproof glass, leaving tiny craters and a network of cracks around them. He saw the gate guard appear and turned his weapon on him. The bullets smashed into the old man, dropping him to the pavement by the gate, his blood beginning to run down the street. The guard never got his pistol clear of his holster.

The remaining three men, still sitting in the limousine, finally sprang into action. The driver threw open his door, ducking low, and moved along the side of the car toward Juana, who stood staring, frozen. He dropped to his hands and knees as bullets whined overhead. He slipped a hand inside his jacket and pulled his pistol, a Browning 9mm.

At the same time, another of the bodyguards sitting in the limo drew his own weapon and began shouting in Spanish, "Juanita, get in. Hurry. Get in."

But the girl was paralyzed with fear. Her eyes were wide, the whites showing around them. Her hands were at her side, and she had let her books fall to the street. She seemed to be staring at the dead men lying near her.

The terrorist with the AK-47 ran around the back of the limo without seeing the bodyguard there. He angled toward the girl, watching her with all his attention.

The limo driver got up to his knees and aimed, squeezing off three rapid shots. The first missed but the second hit the terrorist in the side, just above the belt. It blew out his back, splattering the ground with blood. The third shot clipped him on the opposite side, throwing him to the ground.

As he fell, he pulled the trigger of the AK, stitching the driver from his crotch to his chin, the bullets ripping into him, killing him instantly. He fell back against the side of the car, leaving a red streak on the black paint as he slid to the ground. He was dead as he fell.

Now the terrorist turned his weapon on the men inside, firing through the open rear door. He emptied his magazine, dropped it from the weapon, and slammed another home. The first few rounds blasted into seats. One of the bodyguards died in that hail of bullets, the back of his head blown out, his brains and blood staining the upholstery and splashing across the inside of the windshield.

The girl began to scream then. She made no move to run, to flee. It was as if her feet had grown to the pavement. But she did scream, a continuous wail of pure terror that bordered on panic.

One of the other terrorists ran around the front of the limo, glancing through the windshield at the last living bodyguard who was crouched in the front seat peeking over the top, his pistol in his left hand. The terrorist opened fire, but the glass of the windshield was as impenetrable as that in the side windows. His bullets bounced off. He lowered his weapon and riddled the engine and then the radiator. There was a sound of metal smashing metal and then a bubbling as the radiator ruptured and the water leaked into the street to mingle with the blood of the dead men.

The wounded terrorist kept pouring slugs into the open rear door of the limousine, trying to kill the last bodyguard, who had rolled to the floor to protect himself. He was grazed twice by AK rounds, and one shattered his knee, causing him to shriek in pain.

The terrorist who had disabled the car ran to Juana and grabbed her, trying to pull her with him. She turned her head slowly, staring into his eyes and continuing to scream. She leaned back and set her heels, trying to yank her hand free.

He stopped tugging at her and stepped close. He hit her once in the stomach and she fell to her knees. The man grabbed her under the arms, hauling her to her feet, and finally threw her over his shoulder, carrying her to his Chevy.

Now that the shooting had stopped, they all could hear the wail of a police siren in the far distance. The wounded terrorist had slumped backward, lying prone in the street. He was breathing hard, as if he had just run a long distance. He noticed that the sky seemed to be growing dim, not realizing it was his eyesight failing.

"Help me!" he called softly, speaking almost in a whisper. "I can't make it."

The last of the terrorists, who had been sitting behind the wheel of the Chevy racing the engine without knowing it, got out and stepped up on the rocker panel so he could see his wounded compatriot. Blood had soaked the side of his shirt and stained his trousers. He wasn't looking at anyone.

The driver took out his own pistol, sighted, and fired. The round caught the wounded man in the shoulder, crushing him to the concrete. He rolled to his back, his eyes on the bright blue sky, one hand extended upward as if trying to claw his way to heaven. He moaned once and the driver shot him again, the bullet tearing off the wounded terrorist's chin and then plowing into his chest, killing him.

"Sorry, amigo," said the driver.

The other man tumbled Juana into the back of the Chevy, shoving her to the floor. He forced a pillowcase over her head to blindfold her, and when she tried to protest, he hit her again. He grabbed her arm, forcing it behind her back, jacking her wrist up between her shoulder blades. He pushed her face down.

The driver leaped into the car and dropped it into gear, spinning the wheel. He roared back the way they had come, the police sirens still in the distance. He whipped around a corner and then slowed. He jerked the ski mask from his face and ran a hand through his long, dirty hair, trying to smooth it so that he wouldn't look nearly as wild as he felt.

The girl was whimpering in the back, moaning at the pain in her arm.

The driver turned in his seat, looked at the floor, and reached over, trying to slap her on the head. "Shut her up," he hissed. "Shut her up!"

"Just drive," said the terrorist holding her. He relaxed the pressure on her wrist but grabbed her other arm, pushing it behind her. He lashed her wrists together and then forced her face down so that her head rested on the littered floor. He put his pistol to her head and whispered menacingly, "You shut up or I will shoot you quite dead."

She didn't say anything. She just tried to stop crying and to force the images of men dying and bleeding in the street from her mind. She opened her eyes but saw only the bright white of the pillowcase over her head.

"We did it!" said the man in the back. "I don't believe it, but we did it. We fucking pulled it off."

"Carlos is dead," the driver reminded him.

"Carlos was a fool. I knew he would try a grandstand play. Wanted to be the hero. He was in for self-aggrandizement and not the movement. Well, he got his desire. Now he is a martyr and we can hoist a drink to his memory. He died for the cause. How much farther is it?"

"We'll be at the safe house in just a couple of minutes more."

"Has the communique been sent?"

"Rita should be delivering it right now." The driver snorted. "That should give the pigs something more to think about."

The man in the rear sat back and laced his grubby hands behind his head. Casually he propped his feet up on the bottom of the girl on the floor. "Yeah, something to think about," he said smugly.

2

United States Naval Lieutenant Mark Tynan stepped back and looked at the taut, white silk lean-to constructed from the remains of a parachute and the lines cut from it. The shelter was large enough for two men and had a double layer arrangement to protect those men from the rain and heat of the jungle around them. It wasn't something that Tynan would want to use in Vietnam because the white silk caught and reflected the light, shining like a beacon deep in the jungle. The VC would spot it within minutes, long before a rescue team could get in to extract the downed men—but then Tynan wasn't in Vietnam. He was in Panama, undergoing more survival training that a bureaucrat in Washington had decided that Tynan and his SEAL team needed.

There was a noise behind him, and Tynan turned and saw Boone—one of the enlisted members of his team whom everyone called Dan'l for the obvious reason—coming into the tiny clearing. He was carrying the body of a snake minus the head, part of it looped around his forearm. He held it up, almost as if asking for approval for the kill.

"Goddamned bushmaster," he said. "I don't like snakes any more than Sterne, but this should make a tasty meal. Where are the others?"

"Sterne's out running around in the jungle playing Tarzan and looking for food. Jones was here a minute ago. He's trying to scare up some firewood."

Boone dropped the snake near the shelter and took off his boonie hat so he could wipe the sweat from his forehead. "Christ, Skipper, when we going to get to try something in a cool environment, like Antarctica."

"Because there aren't a whole lot of insurgents in Antarctica," said Tynan, "I wouldn't hold my breath waiting for an assignment there." He stooped and looked at the snake. The head had been lopped off with one clean cut from a machete. He looked up at Boone and asked, "How'd you get this?"

"I was just sitting on a log, minding my own business, when I heard something in the brush. I had stuck my machete in the edge of the log, and when the snake popped into view, I jerked the machete free and chopped off the snake's head. Easy."

At that moment Jones reappeared, carrying a load of wood. He dropped it to the ground near the snake and said, "What the fuck is that?"

"Dinner," said Boone, grinning.

"No way," said Jones. "I'm not eating anything that slithers along the ground."

"Why not?" asked Tynan. "It tastes like chicken."

"Shit!" said Jones. He sat down on the hard-packed earth and picked through the wood. With his knife he began shaving slivers from it to make kindling. "Every time someone wants me to try something disgusting they tell me it tastes like chicken. Rats taste like chicken. Cobra tastes like chicken. Fucking rattlesnakes taste like chicken."

"What're you going to do?" asked Boone, watching Jones prepare his fire. "Rub two sticks together?"

"This is survival training, asshole," said Jones, "not an attempt to re-create the world. We still have matches. I plan to use one to start the fire."

"I would think that in survival training we would want to rub two sticks together," said Tynan.

"Come on, Skipper. Even if we were down somewhere, it wouldn't be like we landed there naked. We would have some equipment. You want to use the flares to start the fire, it's fine with me, but I've got a book of matches here. Nobody said we couldn't use matches if we got them."

Jones finished with the shavings. He scraped a hollow in the dirt and piled the shavings in it. On them he stacked twigs cut from the larger pieces of wood, and over it all he created a pyramid. He checked the wind direction and moved so that he could use his body to shield his match. He struck one and touched the flame to the shavings. They sputtered and popped and began to burn with a flame so light that it was almost impossible to see in the bright afternoon sun. Smoke poured from the top of the pyramid.

"Okay, Smokey the Bear, you got a fire," said Boone. "So what?"

"So now you can cook your chicken-tasting snake," said Jones.

Tynan sat down and began to unlace his boots. There were standard issue in Vietnam, but hard to get in the World. Tynan had brought them with him when he had rotated out of Southeast Asia. He slipped one from his foot and carefully peeled off the thick OD-green, wool sock. He inspected his toes, checking between them, looking for the beginnings of fungus and jungle rot. In the hot and humid environment of the Panamánian jungle it didn't take long for the diseases to set in. It was a constant problem too often ignored by men who hadn't spent much time in the tropics.

Tynan studied his campsite for a moment. There was one large palm tree in the middle of it, and light brush and small bushes around it. A break in the canopy overhead let the sunshine down to the ground so they would have the chance to dry in the warming rays of the sun. Bare earth was visible, some of it because Tynan or one of the men had cut away the vegetation, and some of it occurring naturally. Tynan slipped from the log so that he was seated on the ground, his back against the hardwood and his foot sticking into the sunlight. He wiggled his toes, relaxing.

There was a slight rustling near them, coming from deeper in the jungle. The light breeze wasn't strong enough to create it. Jones looked at Tynan, who was scrambling to get his sock on and his foot stuck back into his boot. It might be a survival exercise, but the Army major running the school wasn't above putting some ''aggressors'' into the field to liven things up for training purposes.

Boone leaped to the side and dodged out of the clearing. He dived under a bush, cursed quietly, but didn't move even though the thorns were tearing at his uniform and exposed skin, and blood began seeping into the scratches.

A second later Sterne appeared. He ran to the fire and kicked it out, grinding the heel of his boot into the dying embers to kill the smoke. To Tynan he said, ''I think someone's coming.''

''So what?'' flared Jones. ''This isn't Vietnam. You didn't have to ruin the fire.''

"I could see the smoke from it for a hundred meters. We don't have to advertise our presence to the enemy, do we?" Sterne shot back.

"You don't know if there is an enemy," countered Jones. "Christ, Sterne, you're a real asshole."

The noise in the jungle came again. Tynan stared toward it, waiting, but heard nothing more. He waved a hand behind him and said, "Let's scatter. Meet at the rendezvous point a hundred meters north of here."

Then, from somewhere in the jungle, they heard, "Lieutenant Tynan? Are you around, sir?"

Tynan looked at Sterne, who still stood with one boot in the remains of the fire, and raised an eyebrow in question.

"Trick?" said Sterne.

"I don't think so." Tynan got to his feet and stamped his foot as if to seat his boot properly. He shrugged and called back, "Over here."

A moment later three men in Army fatigues appeared. They were covered with sweat from their march through the jungle. Each wore a pistol belt with a canteen on each side and a machete in a scabbard, but no pack or knapsack. One had a radio strapped to his back. The leader moved to the log and sat down. He pulled a large OD handkerchief from his pocket and wiped the perspiration from his face. He took off his hat and ran the handkerchief over the short-cropped hair, his elbows on his knees and his eyes on the ground between his feet.

"You need to come in, Lieutenant," said the man. "Commandant sent us out to get you."

"Why?"

"I'm sure that I don't know, sir. He just told us to take a jeep and get in as close as we could. We're parked about an hour from here. We're supposed to bring you back with us. You and your men.''

Tynan looked at his men. Boone was crawling out from under his bush, looking as if he had dived into a cactus patch. Blood was welling from the scratches on his face, his hands, and his arms. Sterne had moved to the right so that he no longer stood in the remains of the fire, and Jones looked frozen as he crouched near the giant palm.

''Take us a couple of minutes to gather the equipment and break the camp,'' said Tynan.

''Don't worry about it, sir,'' said the leader. ''I'll leave my guys here and let them police up the area. I'll come back and get them later.''

By three in the afternoon, Tynan sat in the office of the commandant of the survival school, still wearing his sweat-soaked jungle fatigues and his mud-covered boots. He had tracked through the front office, where the master sergeant sitting behind a fancy wooden desk of teak nearly had a heart attack at the mess left on the floor. He didn't say anything to Tynan, just waved him through.

Tynan entered the office and started to salute the general who sat behind the desk, but the man stood and held a hand out instead. ''Mark Tynan, isn't it?''

Tynan nodded and said, ''Yes, General. United States Navy SEALS.''

The general laughed at that and said, ''Sit down. In a minute or two we'll have a colonel in here to talk to us. He's got a problem that Washington thought you might be able to help him with. I do have a question for you. What in the hell does SEAL stand for?''

"I'm afraid that it's an acronym that somebody in Washington invented in a moment of stupidity. It stands for sea, air, and land, and relates to a seal, which is an animal that is at home in the water and on the land. I guess he thought it was clever, like Seabee. Missed by a little."

The general smiled. "Yeah, by a little. I spent all afternoon trying to figure it out."

Tynan studied the office. He hadn't been in many that belonged to generals or to admirals. He was impressed with the size. It was gigantic. One whole wall, from the floor to the ceiling, was covered with books, thousands of them. It looked like there was everything from military manuals to the latest best-selling fiction. A wall of windows behind the general gave a panoramic view of the jungle that seemed to glow green in the late afternoon sun, and in the distance he could see the top of one of the bridges that crossed the Panama Canal. The other side of the room had a wet bar in one corner and a grouping of furniture that included a long couch and two chairs and might have been a conference area.

Everywhere he looked there was elegance. The woods of the bookcase, desk, doors, and window frames were highly polished. There was a rug on the floor that concealed very little of the glossy hardwood. An air conditioner was hidden somewhere and quietly chugged out cool air while ceiling fans turned slowly overhead.

The general stood and moved toward the bar. "Anything you like while we wait? Mixed drink?"

Tynan wasn't sure of the protocol of the moment. Was he supposed to stand while the general was on his feet? Should he offer to get the drinks even though he didn't know where anything was? Or should he just sit there and keep quiet and hope that the general wasn't protocol happy?

To cover his confusion, Tynan rose and moved so that he could look at the bar. The general had pulled open a couple of doors to reveal nearly every kind of liquor made in the free world.

There was a refrigerator under the bar, and the general opened the door and crouched so that he could look into it. He said, "There's beer in here, if you would prefer it."

"A beer would be very good," said Tynan. "Whatever you have."

Without looking at Tynan, the general held out a green bottle. "This okay?"

"Yes, General," said Tynan. "It's fine." He took the icy bottle.

"Good," said the general, standing up. "I'll have one too." He used a church key to pop the cap and then handed the tool to Tynan.

Tynan opened his beer, set the church key and the cap on the bar, and took a long pull. The beer was nearly ice cold and Tynan thought that his teeth were going to shatter. He felt the liquid seem to pool in his stomach.

The general moved to the conference area and sat down. He was a big man with thick wavy black hair sprinkled with gray. He had a long face with a pointed chin, and his skin was deeply tanned. There were six rows of brightly colored ribbons stacked above his breast pocket and a combat infantryman's badge with a star above them. He looked at his shoes, which shone like black mirrors, and then rubbed the toe of the right one on the back of his trouser leg as if trying to remove a nonexistent speck of dust.

"Tell me about yourself," said the general. He took a drink from his bottle.

Tynan sat opposite the man, took another swig from his beer, and said, "Not much to tell, I'm afraid."

"There must be something," he said. "State is sure high on you. When we called them with our problem and they found out that you were in the area, that was the end of the discussion. They said to give you what you needed and point you in the right direction."

"I've done some work for them in the past," said Tynan, "Although, given the outcome, I don't really understand their enthusiasm."

"Go on."

"Can't really say much about it," said Tynan. "It's classified with a need to know." He sat back then and thought about the mission into Africa. All he had been ordered to do was locate a downed spy plane and blow it up before the Russians found it. That hadn't worked because the Soviets had arrived shortly after Tynan and his team began rigging it for destruction. In the ensuing firefight that took place over several square miles of jungle and ended on a beach, Tynan and his men had killed a number of Soviet soldiers, as well as several locals who were assisting the Russians. On board the retrieval ship, he had been reamed by the CIA case officer sent from London, but the Navy had seemed pleased with the outcome. The plane had been destroyed before the Soviets had a chance to steal any secrets from it. It was nice to know that the work had been appreciated by the bureaucrats even if they hadn't said anything about it.

There was a knock on the door then, and it opened. The master sergeant stuck his head in and announced, "Colonel Watters is here, General."

The general got to his feet and moved across the room. He held out a hand as the colonel entered. "Charlie," he said. "Good to see you again."

"Good to see you, General."

"General? What's this *General* shit? What happened to Dave?"

Watters smiled and said, "When you took off the chickens and put on the general's stars you stopped being Dave and became General."

"Horseshit. I'm still Dave." He turned and pointed at Tynan. "This is the Navy lieutenant that everyone at State said for us to find."

Watters moved across the floor, the leather of his combat boots echoing on the hardwood. He held out a hand and said, "We've got quite a problem for you."

"Sit down. Sit down," said the general. "Charlie, can I get you something to drink?"

"No, I'm fine. Really."

"Okay," said the general. He took his seat, and when everyone seemed comfortable he said, "I suppose we might as well get started. Lieutenant, what do you know about Generalissimo Julio Vasquez y Sanchez?"

Tynan took a sip from his beer and swallowed slowly, thinking. "Let me see. I believe he was the commander of an army or army group or something like that in a Latin American country and decided that he would make a better president than the incumbent president. Engineered a fairly bloodless coup."

"That's pretty close," said Watters, leaning forward. "Where the president had been leaning slightly toward the East, Sanchez is leaning toward the West. The coup was a good thing for us, meaning the United States."

"Okay," said Tynan. "I don't pay much attention to politics in foreign lands."

"That doesn't matter. Something has come up and we are in a position to help Generalissimo Julio Vasquez y Sanchez. State thinks it's a good idea and will help stabilize the region for years to come."

"Colonel," interrupted Tynan, "you don't have to sell me a bill of goods here. Tell me what the job is and I'll let you know if I can help you."

"Fair enough," said Watters. Now he hesitated as if forming the words. He stood and paced to the glass wall and studied the jungle outside. He turned and said, "This isn't really a military matter. It's something that the CIA should handle, and they do have an agent in residence, but if we go sending in CIA agents, things could turn bloody. The CIA isn't very popular in Latin America."

"They're not real popular anywhere," said Tynan, grinning. And I'm getting a little tired of doing their job for them, he thought.

"No, I guess they're not."

"Charlie, you're beating around the bush here. Tell the lieutenant what the trouble is and then we'll learn if he can help us out."

"Right." Watters came back and stopped a couple of feet from Tynan. "The generalissimo has a daughter, Juana Gutierrez, who was going to school in a South American country."

"I thought you said his name was Vasquez y Sanchez," interrupted Tynan.

"Yes. Yes. But the custom is for the daughters to adopt the last name of the mothers and the sons to take both of them, or something like that. I don't fully understand, and besides, that's not the point. The point is, she has been kidnapped."

"Kidnapped?" repeated Tynan.

"That's right," said the general, setting his beer bottle on the floor. "And you have to go find her."

"I don't think that is a job for the Navy. We're not trained in those kinds of matters," Tynan said. "Not at all."

"And I thought that I had made it clear that your opinion has no bearing on the matter," the general reminded him. "You will find her. And you will do it quickly, quietly, and with as little bloodshed as possible."

Tynan could sit still no longer. He got to his feet and walked to the bookcases. For a moment he seemed to study the titles. Finally he turned and said, "General, there must be someone much more qualified for this than me. I'm basically a sailor with a certain expertise in counterinsurgency, but still a sailor."

"Tynan, you're wasting time, and that is something that we don't have a great deal of. The job is yours. You've got it. Period." The general looked at Watters. "Charlie, give it all to him."

"Yes, sir." Watters rubbed his cheek twice and began to talk. He told Tynan all about the kidnapping that left five people dead—three bodyguards, one terrorist, and one old man. One of the bodyguards had survived, though badly wounded, and had provided some information about the kidnapping, the type of car, weapons, and the like. All that had been used to trace the terrorists' path through the city and gave them a couple of clues about the gang's location. A communique had been received from Rita of the Light on the Trail terrorist group, claiming responsibility and demanding the release of seventy-nine prisoners for the safe return of the generalissimo's daughter. They also required the resignation of the new president, Generalissimo Julio Vasquez y Sanchez.

Tynan still didn't understand what it was all about. As near as he could tell, it was something that the FBI should be investigating, although the FBI wasn't authorized to operate outside the United States. The CIA, as an intelligence-gathering organization with agents around the world, might be an even better choice. Tynan said as much.

"The problem with both of those organizations is that it makes the investigation official," said Watters. "If, for some reason, the President would authorize an FBI agent to be assigned to the case, it would give it an official status. The same with the CIA."

"Yes," agreed Tynan, "and if he sends in a naval officer, he has the same problem. The investigation takes on an official status."

"Well," said Watters, "that's not exactly true. The feeling is that a naval officer who happens to be vacationing in South America is a lot less conspicuous than an FBI or CIA agent suddenly appearing on the scene. Too many awkward questions might be asked if one of them suddenly appeared."

"I would want a recon of the area," said Tynan, thinking out loud. "I want to go and look at the kidnap site and talk to the surviving bodyguard. I want the complete text of the communique you mentioned."

"I can see no reason for that," said Watters.

"If the lieutenant wants the information and wants to see the site, then I don't think we should stand in his way," said the general. He looked at Tynan. "When can you be ready to leave?"

"Probably sometime tomorrow. Noon or a little after, depending on the flights scheduled out of here."

Watters looked into his folder and said, "We do have a deadline. One week from the time of the kidnapping, which was yesterday afternoon. At that time, if the generalissimo hasn't resigned or if the arrangements for it haven't been made, they are going to kill his daughter and have threatened to take other members of his family hostage."

"That's fucking great," said Tynan. He held out his hand and said, "Give me the file. I'll want to study it. And anything else that might prove useful."

"It's all classified information," said Watters. "There's a lot of stuff from confidential sources about the Light on the Trail terrorist group. We don't want that to get out. It could compromise our sources."

"I'm not going to sell it to the Russians," snapped Tynan. "I can't work in the dark on this. I need all the information available on it."

The general nodded at Watters and said, "Give him everything he wants."

"General, that's not good military procedure," said Watters quietly.

"Neither is sending a Navy lieutenant out to do a job for the CIA, but that's what's happening, so give him the fucking file and anything else that he wants."

"Yes, sir."

"Tynan," said the general, "you check with my aide tomorrow at zero eight hundred. He'll make your flight arrangements. At that time you'll have to tell him what else you'll want and who else you'll want with you."

"Yes, sir," said Tynan, getting to his feet. "I'm not sure about this. Not at all."

"You'll do just fine, Lieutenant," said the general.

3

After the meeting with General McKibben and the colonel, Tynan found his men at a back table of one of the beer clubs scattered through the Canal Zone complex. Tynan worked his way through the maze of tables, chairs, and benches and sat down on the hard wooden chair left vacant for him. The top of the table was scarred by the initials of a hundred different GIs who had been in the bar during the last decade. A pitcher of beer sat on the table along with four glasses. Three of them had been used and the fourth was waiting for Tynan. He poured himself a beer, drank half of it, and then set the glass down.

The club was dimly lit and filled with cigarette smoke. A bar dominated one wall, and there was a single bartender and three cocktail waitresses who wore short skirts and fishnet stockings. Rock music blared from a stereo jukebox crouching near the bar, making conversation difficult.

Jones leaned across the table and shouted at Tynan, "I think I love the brunette."

"Yeah," said Sterne. "She smiled at him and now he thinks she loves him too."

Tynan turned and searched the crowd until he found the waitress Jones loved. She had very long hair that reached to her waist, long shapely legs, and large firm breasts that strained the fabric of her

23

blouse. Her face was thin and her chin slightly pointed. Her eyes were large and dark.

Over his shoulder he said, "A good choice, Jones. A very good choice."

Boone grabbed the empty pitcher and banged it on the table. "Why don't you get your girlfriend to give us another one," he said.

Without a word Jones grabbed the pitcher and got to his feet. He walked over to the waitress, waited while she took another table's order, and then leaned close to whisper in her ear.

Everyone watched as she laughed and put the empty pitcher on her tray. She moved the damp towel out of the way and pushed the tiny cashbox to the side. She stood talking to Jones for several minutes, laughed once or twice, and then headed for the bar.

Jones strolled back, hands in his hip pockets. He sat down slowly, grinning, and said, "She'll bring us a pitcher in a minute."

"You spent quite a bit of time talking to her," said Sterne. "What was that all about?"

Before Jones could reply, Tynan jumped in and said, "We've got a couple of things to discuss and Jones's love life is not among them."

All the men suddenly fell silent. When the new pitcher appeared, Boone poured a beer for each of them.

Tynan leaned forward conspiratorily, his elbows on the table. He lowered his voice so that it was barely audible to the men at the table with him and masked from the surrounding people by the rocking beat from the jukebox. "We've been given another assignment," he told them, "though I don't know why they selected us. It's the reason we were pulled from the exercise earlier today."

"What is it?" asked Sterne.

Tynan looked into the face of the man. Sterne was one of the older of the SEALS, maybe twenty-five. He was of medium height and weight, with dark hair. His skin was deeply tanned from his recent stints in the tropics. He had light-colored eyes that seemed almost washed out; they might have been blue or gray, or a little of both. He was very good in the field—anything from open desert to tropical rain forest—and able to move through the roughest country rapidly without making a sound. That made him a near-perfect point man. He had been with Tynan for the final exam, which was an ambush in Vietnam, and after that he had become a permanent part of Tynan's team, as had Boone.

Quickly Tynan outlined the problem. A kidnapping where the victim was the daughter of a friend of the United States. They had to go get her.

Sterne was the first to speak. "Fuck it, Skipper," he said. "We're not cops."

"That was my reaction," said Tynan. "Exactly. But let me put it to you the way the general put it to me. Everyone thinks it would be a good idea if we looked into this. And we haven't been asked for an opinion."

"Ah," said Boone. "So when do we start?"

"Tomorrow," said Tynan. "I want you guys to start looking into securing equipment. I'm not sure exactly what we're going to need, but I would suggest getting with the MPs or the Security Police and seeing if any of them have an idea. Since this is going to be basically a police operation, we'll want to adopt a police point of view."

"That seems like a good question, Skipper," said Boone. "If this is a police operation, why not send in MPs or the CID or OSI instead of us?"

"Apparently someone in State was impressed with our handling of the crashed plane and remembered our names. It's an outgrowth of that."

"Fucking wonderful," said Sterne.

"My reaction exactly," said Tynan. He got to his feet and said, "I've got some studying to do tonight, so I'll punch out now. I'll check with you in the morning, after I meet with the general's aide. See you then."

When Tynan was gone, Sterne asked, "Anybody have any idea on how to proceed from here?"

"It would seem to me," said Boone, "we do what the skipper said. Talk to the MPs about it. Maybe they'll have an idea. They are cops."

Jones picked up his beer and drained half the glass. "I've got to get going too," he said.

"Get going too!" said Sterne. "Where the fuck are you going?"

"Julie gets off now." Jones pointed at the bar, where the long-haired waitress that Jones claimed he loved was giving her tray to another waitress.

"Christ! You're kidding," said Boone as he turned in his seat to look over his shoulder. "You've really got a date with her?"

"Yup!" said Jones, getting to his feet. "I'm walking her home, and then we just might hit the NCO Club over at Howard. She's in the Air Force and lives on the base."

"I don't believe it," said Sterne. "I just don't fucking believe it. How'd you do it?"

"We're from the same hometown," said Jones. "Gets them every time."

Sterne shook his head as he stared at the tabletop, picking at a napkin he held there. "I don't get it. How'd you know that she was from your hometown?"

Jones slopped a little beer from the pitcher in his empty glass, chugged it down, and said, "You have to ad-lib a little, for Christ's sake."

"I think I'm going to be sick to my stomach," said Sterne quietly.

Tynan sat in his room in the Visitor Officer's Quarters and read everything that was in the file Watters had given to him. The room wasn't much to look at. There was an old settee against one wall, the fabric frayed and faded. A low pine coffee table sat in front of it, and beside it was a refrigerator with the noisiest compressor in the free world.

Tynan got up and moved to the window and turned down the air conditioner that had been rattling there. He was tempted to turn on the nineteen-inch black and white TV with its bent rabbit ears wrapped in aluminum foil, but resisted. There was nothing on that he really wanted to watch.

He returned to the settee and sat down. He picked up the folder and began reading again. The file told him little that would be of help to him.

The Light on the Trail terrorist organization was a fairly new one. No one really knew who the leaders were or what they wanted, although in the few communiques they had released they called for land reform, the release of political prisoners, a disbanding of the government, and an end to the capitalistic system.

"Sounds communist to me," said Tynan out loud.

The file also told him that the terrorists' major targets had been generating plants, American corporate branches, and airline offices. They had blacked out the capital city twice by blowing up a hydroelectric dam and a relay station, but no one had been injured in any of the bombings or attacks. It seemed that they were stepping up their activities.

But the problem with all the information was that it was yesterday's news. Reports of the terrorists' claims that were a year old. Speculation that they would hit the generating plant at Rio del Norte on Tuesday, or that Monday was a holiday among the terrorists' groups and they would celebrate with some kind of newsmaking attack.

Tynan closed the folder and tossed it to the table. He leaned back, his head against the flimsy wall, and closed his eyes. There was nothing in the file that would help him. No names of terrorists. No locations where they might be found. Nothing. Just a list of things they had done and attacks they might make in the future.

Suddenly he realized that he was at a complete loss. He had no idea of what was next, what to do. He had not been trained to investigate a kidnapping. Blow up a coastal installation, infiltrate the enemy lines, assassinate the communist leaders of the Viet Cong, fight a war of counterinsurgency, but not investigate a kidnapping.

He got up and walked around the room again. He touched the top of the desk set under the window that was hidden behind rubberized curtains and venetian blinds. He walked back toward the refrigerator and opened it, but there was nothing in it except a half-used jar of French's mustard. He stood there, one arm on the door and the other across the top, staring at the interior as his mind raced.

And the only thing he could think of was that he was out of his depth. He was not a cop, and that was what he was supposed to become. But being a cop was something he knew very little about. Some cops bragged about never having to draw a weapon or shoot at people, and Tynan had drawn his weapon frequently. He just wasn't comfortable with the concept of a police operation.

At eight o'clock the next morning, Tynan, dressed in civilian clothes, was standing in the master sergeant's office, waiting for General McKibben's aide, Captain Roy Belcher, to arrive. The door to Belcher's office opened and Belcher waved Tynan in.

"Sit down, Mark," said Belcher. "You don't mind if I call you Mark, do you?"

"No, of course not." Tynan sat down in one of the two chairs near the desk. The office wasn't much more than a cubicle. The walls were bare except for a single print that was labeled "The Wagon Box Fight." A small window behind the desk looked out on the jungle.

"Before we start," said Tynan, "I'd better give you this." He held up the manila folder with the classified information about the Light on the Trail in it.

Belcher took it and locked it in the safe in the corner of his office. "Now," said Belcher, sitting down behind the desk. "I've got your tickets and hotel reservations for you. You take off at nine-thirty and land incountry at one. You'll be met at the airport and driven to the International House Hotel." He pushed an envelope across the desk.

"This hardly sounds like the low-key incountry recon that Watters and the general were talking about last night," commented Tynan.

"At this late date I had to pull some strings to get the flight and the hotel space. I was told that it was imperative that you get into the country and the hotel."

Tynan nodded and asked, "Anything else come in during the night? Anything I should know about?"

"No, not a thing."

"Okay," said Tynan, "there is one other item. I want a pistol, preferably a Browning M-35 9mm, but I'll take whatever is available. Somebody is going to have to make arrangements for me to get through customs with the weapon."

Belcher held up a hand as if to halt him. "We can't get anything through customs, and to force the issue would be like tying a red flag to your coat-tails. No, what you'll have to do is go to the American Embassy in Quito. The military attache or the commander of the Marine guard will provide you with the weapon. It'll be potluck on that, I'm afraid."

They went on like that for another fifteen minutes, Belcher adding more and more information and Tynan listening to him. Finally, as Belcher began to repeat himself, Tynan stood up. There was nothing more he wanted to say to the general's aide. Or hear from him. He plucked the tickets off the desk and slipped them into the inside pocket of his sport coat. "Thank you, Captain," he said.

"Good luck to you," said Belcher.

When he left Belcher's office, he glanced at his watch and realized that he had very little time. He needed to pick up his suitcase at the VOQ, get to the terminal building at Howard to check through customs, and then board the airplane. He had little more than an hour to accomplish it all.

Outside, he climbed into the jeep that he had been given for the morning. He drove to the enlisted men's quarters at Howard, wondering why his men had been put into an Air Force dormitory, but deciding that it wasn't worth the effort to worry about. It might have been the only space available at that moment, so the Navy used it.

The dormitories were multistoried affairs with open hallways around the outside. Tynan entered through a set of double glass doors, climbed up the steps to the third floor, and then walked down the hall. He passed a half dozen machines that dispensed beer and Coke and candy. There was a communal latrine and he saw a couple of men, towels wrapped around their waists, shaving or brushing their teeth. Halfway down the hall, he found Jones's room and knocked on the door. When there was no answer he knocked again, hard, and heard an irritated and muffled response from the inside.

"Yeah. Yeah. I'm awake. Hold your bladder."

A second later the door opened and Jones stood there in his underwear, his hair sticking up at all angles and a puffy look to his face. There was a bright red crease along his cheek where the edge of the pillow had been. Jones didn't look up, but stared at the waxed cement floor as if the bright sunlight from the outside was impossible to take so early.

Tynan stepped closer and pushed on the door as if to open it wider. He wanted to talk to Jones before the flight. "You going to invite me in?" asked Tynan.

Jones didn't move immediately. He looked back over his shoulder and then shrugged.

Inside the darkened room, Tynan saw a shape move on the bed and then sit up. The sheet fell away, and Tynan could see the barmaid that Jones had claimed he loved.

She was naked to the waist. She sat on the bed, the sheet wrapped around her legs. She ran a hand through the tangle of brown hair and then slowly turned toward the door. When she saw Tynan she said "Oh" in a quiet voice. She then fell back on the bed and pulled the sheet over her head as if to hide. The motion freed one corner, revealing one of her ankles and part of her calf.

Now Jones stepped back to let Tynan enter. "What's the problem, Skipper?"

"No problem. My flight leaves in about forty-five minutes. I thought I should warn one of you guys about that and tell you that I still don't know what the hell we're doing. Just follow the plan from last night—that is, talk to the MPs and anyone else you can think of. And tell Sterne to look into securing some weapons for us. Maybe some of the antiterrorist guidelines being developed will be helpful with that. Look to outfit us for a week in the field."

Jones looked over his shoulder at the shape on his bed. He could see her fingertips where they clutched the sheet over her head. "Should you be talking like this?" he whispered. "I mean out here in the open?"

"I haven't said anything yet," laughed Tynan. "I don't know when I'll be back, but you'll have to be ready to move at a moment's notice. You'll have to tell Captain Belcher—he's General McKibben's aide—where you are so that I'll be able to find you easily, if I have to. Tell Boone and Sterne the same thing. That I want them handy."

"Sure, Skipper."

"Right. Well, I've got to get going. I'll see you in a couple of days at the most." He leaned past Jones and raised his voice. "It was nice seeing you," he said to the shape hidden on the bed.

For a moment there was no response, and then he heard an explosion of laughter as the bed began to shake.

Back downstairs, Tynan climbed into his jeep and drove to his quarters to pick up his suitcase. He scanned the room quickly to make sure that he was leaving nothing that he would need soon, checked the bathroom, and then left. He didn't check out, figuring that he could use the room when he returned, whenever that might be. From there he drove to the terminal and left the jeep parked in front.

Inside, his luggage was inspected by a bored Air Force NCO and a tired customs agent. They passed him, making a chalk checkmark on his suitcase, made him walk through a jury-rigged metal detector that was the result of the latest round of commercial aircraft hijackings, and then had nothing to do with him.

Within minutes he was on board the jet and it was rolling down the runway. The plane leaped into the sky, climbed out over the Gulf of Panama, and then turned due south, flying over part of the Pacific Ocean, skirting along the coast of Colombia. Periodically, through the windows, Tynan could catch a glimpse of the coast, the Andes rising rapidly in background, covered with a deep green. There were clouds, dark and menacing, building over the mountains, and Tynan couldn't help thinking that they somehow looked ominous.

They finally crossed the coastline on the trip to Quito. Far below, Tynan could see the browns of the beaches, the greens of farmers' fields, and finally the deep verdant color of jungle. In a few minutes, the plane was touching down in the capital of Ecuador. Tynan wasn't sure what his first move was going to be. He had worried about it during the fairly short flight and had thought of nothing. All he could do was hang loose, as he had often advised his men to do, and play the situation by ear.

4

High in the mountains to the east of Quito was a single stone and thatch structure that dominated a large field of grass and wildflowers. A winding dirt path led to a rough wood door flanked by two glass-less windows. A man dressed in patched pants and a frayed cotton shirt dug lazily at a weed-overrun garden. He didn't seem to be too interested in what he was doing, because he kept stopping to gaze at the mountains behind him or the trees a couple of hundred meters in front of him.

The inside of the hut contained two rooms and a closet. In the front room was a table made from scrap lumber, surrounded by four broken-down chairs. A cracked ceramic basin had been built along one wall, and torn, dirty curtains hung beneath it.

Two men sat playing cards at the table in the front room. Next to one of them was a rifle with a small scope on it. The other wore a shoulder holster containing an American-made .357 Magnum. In the corner were two automatic rifles, both manufactured in the Soviet Union.

The second room contained a large bed with a quilt used as a bedspread on it. There was nothing else and no one else in the room.

It was the closet that was interesting. Inside, on the floor of compressed dirt that had been swept clean by the former owner of the cabin—now buried along with his wife and two children in an unmarked grave in a stand of trees—was Juana Gutierrez. She was naked, her clothes having been ripped and cut from her moments after they had arrived at the hut. Her hands were bound behind her and a rope around her elbows drew them painfully close together. Her ankles and knees were also tied together, and a rope from her knees wrapped around her neck so that she was sitting with her thighs pressed against her breasts.

She had been beaten twice since they had arrived at the cabin. The first time was just after they had cut her clothes from her, leaving the pillowcase fastened over her head and her hands tied tightly behind her. They had punched her in the stomach and kicked her in the ribs when she fell to the floor. They had pushed her into a chair and hit her in the face and breasts, keeping at it until she moaned continuously and finally lost all consciousness. When she came to, she had been in the dark closet and had no idea of where she was. Her body ached from the beating and her hands and feet were cold because of the bonds.

Later she had been dragged from the closet, at first blinded by the bright light from the windows as they jerked the pillowcase from her head. One man had untied her ankles and then stood up in front of her. He grinned at her and then hit her as hard as he could in the stomach.

She dropped as if she had been shot, trying to breathe with lungs that seemed paralyzed. She rolled to her side, hiking her knees up, her mouth working rapidly as a curtain of black descended from above. Slowly the black dissipated and she sucked in air greedily.

They stood her up and began to beat her methodically with wooden dowels nearly an inch thick. They hit her thighs, arms, stomach, and chest. The beating left her covered with thick red welts that turned black and blue and saffron and hurting. Each breath seemed to be a new level in pain, and she was sure they had broken a couple of her ribs.

The only thing that she had to hold on to was that they hadn't raped her yet. They had threatened rape and had actually probed her crotch with one of the dowels, but she had been beaten to a state of semi-consciousness and was only vaguely aware of what was happening. When she failed to respond the way they thought she should, they tied her ankles again and pushed her back into the closet.

Now she sat in the dark praying that someone would rescue her but knowing it wouldn't happen. No one knew where she was, or in what country, or even on what continent. She tried to keep the hopelessness out of her mind, but it kept intruding like an unwanted relative. She would have cried if she had had any tears left, but she had cried herself out hours ago, or days ago, or weeks ago. She didn't even know how long she had been held captive. Only that the men had seemed to enjoy their work as they hit her and watched her writhe in pain.

Tynan was hurried through the terminal and customs and out into the parking lot where a black limousine waited, the pennants of the American Embassy flapping in the light breeze of the early afternoon. Tynan was surprised by the change in temperature. In Panama it had been hot and humid, and here it was warm and dry. Cumulus clouds were piling up over the mountains to the south and east and threatened rain later in the day, but as Tynan stepped into the parking lot, there was bright sunshine.

As he appeared, the door of the limousine opened and a man in light suit got out and waved at Tynan. He then came forward and tried to take the suitcase from Tynan's hand.

"Wish you people hadn't bothered with meeting me in a limousine," said Tynan.

"We were told what flight you were on, what you looked like, and to meet you here," said the man. "I was only following my orders."

"And identifying me as an important person with some kind of political clout for anyone who cares to notice," said Tynan. "Not exactly the low profile that I had hoped to maintain as I arrived incountry."

The man ignored the criticism as he opened one of the rear doors of the car. He let Tynan climb in the back and said, "It'll take us a few minutes to arrive at the embassy. Sit back and enjoy the ride. You'll find the bar well stocked, but the English-language TV station doesn't begin broadcasting until early in the evening."

Tynan couldn't shake the feeling that the man was issuing him orders. Enjoy the ride. Look at the scenery. Use the bar. Tynan turned and looked at the rear window and saw the man open the trunk long enough to stash his suitcase. He then got into the front with the driver and nodded to him. They lurched off without another word.

As promised, the trip to the embassy didn't take long. Tynan had no real chance to get the feel of Quito. He knew that it had once belonged to the Incan Empire, and there was evidence of that influence in some of the stone masonry around him. He saw people dressed much in the same way that they did in the other cities of the world. There were small shops that specialized in handcrafts, metals, glass, and rugs woven from fabric made from llama wool, and there were offices with big windows displaying scenes from around the world, there were high-rise buildings and cardboard shanties. Like most of the Third World, Quito was a city of extreme contrasts.

At the embassy, Tynan was escorted inside, past the reception area with its ornate desk, large waiting room, and blond American secretary. He was hustled up a wide flight of stairs and down a long wide hallway, past closed offices that had no names on the doors, past others that boasted the charge d'affaires and passport control and visas. The man from the limousine opened an unmarked door and stood back so that Tynan could enter.

"Lieutenant Colonel Jonathan Wilson will be with you shortly," said the man from the limousine. "You may wait in here."

Tynan entered to find a long-haired brunette sitting behind a small wooden desk. She wore huge oval glasses that hid her eyes. She smiled at Tynan with teeth that were slightly yellowed, and Tynan could see a pack of cigarettes sitting near the phone on her desk. She was a slender girl who looked no more than twenty-one.

"Please have a seat," she said in a voice that was an octave lower than most women spoke. "The colonel will be right with you."

Tynan thanked her and sat down, looking at the mint copies of *Time* and *Newsweek* and *Field and Stream*. He didn't pick up any of the magazines. He watched the secretary, whose name was Suzy Hamilton according to the nameplate on her desk, type a letter. Then he looked out the window and could see the mountains of the Andes towering over them.

In a moment the door to the inner office opened and a tall thin man with absolutely no hair on his head, not even eyebrows, looked out. He wore a white shirt that was damp under the arms even though it wasn't that warm, and light gray trousers. He glanced at Tynan and waved him up. To Hamilton he said, "Hold my calls for the next twenty minutes or so. Unless Franklin calls. Put him through."

"Yes, sir."

Tynan followed Wilson through the door. Wilson closed it and pointed to one of the leather chairs sitting in front of his desk. "Sit, Mark, isn't it?"

"Mark will be fine, Colonel." Tynan thought that he was seeing quite a few offices in the last few days and beginning to understand the psychology of the selection of offices. This one was larger than Belcher's, but then Belcher was only an Army captain, the same rank as Tynan. Wilson was a lieutenant colonel with a fairly important job, so his office was bigger than Belcher's. It had two new leather armchairs near a big desk that was mahogany or teak or some other dark wood. A judge's chair sat behind it and a large window was behind the chair. There was a couch and a coffee table along one wall and a bookcase next to it containing only a hundred books, many of them about Ecuador and the Incas. None of it was nearly as impressive as McKibben's office in Panama, but then McKibben was a general. Wilson did have all the same items as McKibben, but there were fewer of them and they were smaller and older.

Wilson walked around the desk, spun the chair so that he could sit, and then, leaning forward on his desk that held a red felt blotter, a pen and pencil set, and a single In basket, he said, "What can I do for you?"

"First, I assume, since I was met at the airport, that you've received some kind of message about me."

"Correct."

"Then you know that I'm looking for a weapon."

Wilson leaned back and tented his fingers under his chin. It was almost as if he was withdrawing from an unpleasant conversation. "I have received a missive that suggests I should cooperate with you and that you requested a Browning 9mm pistol."

"Then you have it?" asked Tynan.

"Let me be frank with you, Mark. I'm not inclined to hand out weapons to anyone who comes in here and asks for one. If you're armed, then you are just that much more likely to get into trouble. You believe that you are carrying an equalizer, that with the pistol you are invincible. You create a poor image for our Latin American brothers and endless paperwork for us here at the embassy."

Now it was Tynan who leaned forward, his elbows on his knees. He was taking control of the situation, establishing his dominance over it. He said, "I didn't know the point was open for discussion. I was told that the weapon would be here for me when I arrived."

"There are weapons here, in the building," said Wilson noncommittally.

"Fine. I would like to have one and a sufficient supply of ammunition for it. Say fifty rounds. If you have the Browning, make it four spare magazines."

Wilson dropped his hands to his desktop so that only the fingertips showed. "That seems like an excessive amount of ammo. Are you planning to start a war?"

"Colonel Wilson, I don't have time to get into a debate. I have been given an assignment that has a

very short fuse on it. Your people may have already
compromised it by showing up at the airport with a
fucking limousine. Now, please get my weapon and
tell me how I can get a car.''

''We have plenty of cars here. I'll have one assigned to you immediately.''

''Does it have embassy plates on it? Embassy
markings?'' asked Tynan tiredly.

''Of course.''

''Then why don't I just take out an ad in the paper and then put on a beacon so that the opposition
can spot me without any trouble.''

For a moment Wilson said nothing. The look on
his face said that he didn't like Tynan and that he
would be happier if Tynan would just disappear. Finally he said, ''I'll have one of the embassy Marines bring a weapon up. Now, there are a couple
of places to get a car if you feel you need one and
don't want one of ours. You'll need to supply your
American driver's license and show them your passport. They may try to get you to leave your passport
to ensure that you bring the car back, but under no
circumstances surrender it to them.''

''I understand.''

''We have booked a room for you at the International. But the embassy is connected to that, so
you might want to make your own arrangements.''

Tynan rubbed a hand through his hair and studied
the floor. For the first time he saw the intricate pat-
tern woven into the rug.

His mind raced. He was already linked to the embassy and if he didn't take the room, it might look
like he was trying to duck the notoriety. Once he
left the hotel, he could drop from sight easily, and
he didn't plan to use the room longer than one night
anyway.

He looked up and said, "No, I'll use the room."

Wilson nodded, picked up his phone, punched a button, and spoke quickly and quietly. He hung up carefully, studying the phone. Without looking at Tynan he said, "Your weapon and ammo will be here in a moment, Lieutenant. Now, if you have nothing else, I really must get back to work. The Marine will meet you in the outer office."

Tynan rose and waited to see what Wilson would do, but the colonel was suddenly engrossed in the file sitting on the red blotter, flipping through it quickly. Without another word, Tynan left the office. He closed the door softly and then looked at Hamilton. She had turned her chair so that she was facing the typing table, her hands on the keyboard, and from his angle, Tynan could see that she was wearing a short skirt. He studied her legs for a moment before moving around to the front of her desk.

"I've a question for you," he said.

She continued typing for a second, finishing the line, and then turned to face him. "Yes?"

When she turned, Tynan noticed that the top two buttons on her blouse were undone and he could see her breasts and her dark lacy bra. He tried not to stare and said, "This may sound a little strange, but I was wondering . . ."

"Why, Lieutenant," she said as a huge smile spread across her face, "I thought you'd never ask."

Without thinking about it, he said, "No, you misunderstand. I need to know if there is a seedy section of town. Bars and the like where the people, the natives, hang out."

She lowered her eyes and the smile died on her face. "Yes. It's not hard to find."

Suddenly Tynan realized what was happening. He said, "Listen, ah . . ." He glanced at the nameplate again. "Suzy, I'm sorry, but I have business that just can't wait."

"Sure. I understand. The Marines will have the information that you want," she said coldly.

At that moment the door opened and a Marine sergeant entered. He asked, "Lieutenant Tynan?"

"Yes."

He held out a small package. "We had the Browning but only three spare magazines."

Tynan took it and said, "Thanks." He shot a glance at Hamilton, who was suddenly looking at him with a different expression on her face. Tynan said to her, "It was nice meeting you."

She had softened when she saw the Marine hand Tynan the weapon. She said, "Nice to meet you too."

"Now, Sergeant," said Tynan as he opened the door, "I've a couple of questions to ask you."

5

As Tynan left his dormitory room, Jones closed the door and turned to look at the woman who was hiding under the covers. She pulled the sheet down to her chin, searched the room as if looking for spies, and then sat up. The sheet dropped to her waist and she swung her feet to the floor. She sat up, remaining motionless for a moment as if she had just awakened and wasn't sure of her next move.

"Sorry about that," Jones said to her. "I didn't know that the skipper was going to stop by this morning."

"Is this going to cause you any trouble with your boss?" she asked.

"No," said Jones, shaking his head. "The skipper understands. Besides, I wouldn't be surprised to learn that he had company last night too."

She ran her hand through her long hair until it became too entangled to move. She pulled at the snarls and said, "You should have let me braid it last night. It's going to take an hour to comb it out."

Jones leaned against the door, his arms folded across his chest and his ankles crossed. He surveyed the woman carefully. She was naked except for a bit of sheet wrapped around her waist. She wasn't looking at him but at her long brown hair, pulling and picking at it. Jones knew that she had dark sultry eyes. He

44

watched her hand with its long thin fingers and short bitten nails. He let his eyes fall to her slim ankles and the rounded calves and slowly raised them, staring at her legs. They were as shapely now, sitting on the bed, as they had been when encased in the black fishnets that were part of her cocktail waitress costume.

"Damn!" she said sharply. "Damn and double damn. I just knew it."

Jones picked up the comb that was lying on the side of the sink slipped into one corner of the room under a cracked mirror. He knee-walked across the bed until he was directly behind her. "Let me help," he said.

"Sure," she said. "Please do." She pushed the sheet to the floor and sat on it. She had folded her legs under her, Indian fashion.

Jones looked over her shoulder, down her soft taut belly, to the dark patch between her legs. He gulped once and then leaned back so that he couldn't see anything except her hair. He sat on the edge of the bed, his knees beside her shoulders, her long hair draped across his leg so that he could drag his comb through it.

Slowly he worked his way through her hair, starting near the ends of it and progressing carefully to the crown of her head so that he was combing it out in long, cautious swipes. He worked on it as the morning passed and the men in the building got up to return to their military jobs. He kept at it as the maids cleaned their way through the whole dorm and knocked on his door, demanding that they be allowed to finish his room. He kept at it until her hair had become silky and flowing, and she leaned her head against him and purred deep in her throat.

"You know," she said, "I think this turns me on quicker than about anything."

Jones kissed the top of her head and said, ''What turns you on?''

''Having someone comb my hair for me.'' She slipped an arm over one of his legs, almost as if she was afraid he would get away. ''It's such a luxurious feeling, I guess. I have nothing to do but let someone else comb my hair.''

Jones dropped the comb to the bed and rubbed her bare shoulder. When she turned her head to look back at him, he leaned forward and kissed her, forcing his tongue into her mouth. He let his hand dip lower until his index finger touched her nipple. He massaged it and felt it expand, stiffening.

She pulled away and said breathlessly, ''You keep that up for very long and we're not going to get out of here until after nightfall.''

''That works for me,'' said Jones. He slipped his hands under her arms and lifted her to her feet and then stood with her, turning her, pressing himself against her.

It was at that moment someone knocked on the door.

''What?'' snapped Jones, exasperated.

''Tom? Open up? We've got work to do.''

''I think everyone around here hates us.'' She giggled. ''Give me a second to get a shirt or something on and then you can open the door.

Jones grabbed a pair of camouflage fatigue pants and put them on, buckling the belt but not zipping the fly. He stepped to the door and put a hand on the knob.

''I'm set,'' she said.

Jones opened the door and saw Boone standing there. Behind him, staring at the open field that was crisscrossed with paths, was Sterne.

Boone pushed by, saw the woman standing in the room wearing only a fatigue jacket that covered her as completely as her cocktail costume, stopped, and said, "Pardon me."

"Dan'l," said Jones, "I'd like you to meet Julie Kincaid. Julie, this is one of my teammates. We call him Dan'l in honor of his last name which is Boone, but I don't think he's related to the real one. And standing in the door is Sterne. I never call him anything but Sterne. I think his first name is something strange like Alphous."

"We'll wait outside," said Boone. "We've got a meeting with the provost marshal at Fort Clayton at eleven."

Jones closed the door and said, "What time do you have to be to work?"

Julie shrugged. "This is my day off from my Air Force job. I've got to be to the club by six."

"If you'd like," said Jones, "I'll walk you back to your quarters."

"No," she said. "That's okay. Really. I'll wait here for a little while, wash up, and then head on back. You coming by tonight?"

"I don't know." Jones shrugged. "I really don't know what we're going to run into at the provost marshal's office. Depending on that, I'll be by if I can."

She unbuttoned the fatigue jacket and let it fall open. She shrugged her shoulders so that the jacket slipped to the floor and she stood in front of him naked. She stepped close to him and kissed him and said, "Do what you can."

The provost marshal sat behind a scarred, battleship gray desk that looked as if it had first been used during the Civil War. He had a chair that squeaked every time he moved, which was frequently. He was a big man with thick dark hair and a beard that grew in heavy and black so that his cheek and chin had a bluish color.

"Now," he said, his voice booming at them. "What can I do for you fellows?"

Boone rubbed his chin several times before responding. "I'm afraid that I'm not sure."

"Well, that certainly narrows it down, doesn't it?" The provost marshal grinned. "Maybe you could be just a little more specific."

"We have a problem," said Sterne, taking over for Boone. "We have to ask some questions, but the nature of the matter is confidential."

"You don't have to worry about me carrying tales out of school," said the PM.

Sterne outlined the problem quickly, and then explained what they needed to know. He mentioned briefly the kidnapping and that they had been charged with finding the terrorists. "Our problem is that we don't know how to proceed."

"Uh-huh," said the provost marshal. "Let me ask you a question. The victim was in one country and her father is in another, and neither of those countries is the one where we are now?"

"That about covers it," said Sterne, grinning.

"Then you don't have a prayer. You have nowhere to begin, can't go anywhere, and have no place to stand. It's a ridiculous assignment."

"But it's the one we've been given," protested Sterne.

"Then you have an impossible task," said the man. "I mean, the first thing you would do is put a tap on the victim's family's phone, but you can't do that. You can't even interview the victim's family. Do you know who the victim is? Do you have a photograph?"

Jones shook his head. "We're completely out of our depth here."

The provost marshal stood up so that he could escort them out of the office. "I'm afraid that there isn't much I can do for you fellows. There's just no way to begin an investigation like this. No way at all."

The first thing Tynan did after he secured the rental car—a rusting old Plymouth that ran rough, backfired all the time, and threatened to die at every intersection—was drive to the scene of the kidnapping. He cruised past the school's entrance slowly, the evidence of the firefight covered by new cement that barely disguised the pockmarks on the stone pillars of the black iron gate. There were clean spots on the street where the bloodstains had been sandblasted away.

Tynan turned around and drove by again. Now, in the bushes and rubber trees that marked the perimeter of the school, he could see a second, hidden guard box. The iron gate looked new and seemed to have been constructed of rolled steel bars. There was a massive lock on it and braces that were anchored solidly in the concrete.

As he passed the gate a second time, a guard dressed in a spotless khaki uniform left the protection of another newly erected hut. He carried a stubby looking submachine gun that could have been an Israeli Uzi. He held it casually in both hands, the barrel pointing in the general direction of Tynan's car. Tynan decided that he had seen enough at the ambush site. The place had been effectively cleaned and repaired, and the new guards were there for more than just show.

Tynan stepped on the gas, increasing his speed. In the rearview mirror he could see the guard studying the back of his vehicle as if attempting to get the license number, so he could report the activity to the local police.

Tynan drove back to the center of the town and then began to orbit outward, studying the streets and the life on them, trying to get a feeling for the local population. Once away from the center of the town, he found himself among one- or two-story buildings made of crumbling stone and rotting lumber. The pavement, where there was any, was cracked and disintegrating. Where there was no pavement, there was hard-packed dirt that was rutted and littered with holes, with shoulders that disappeared into the weeds that lined it.

Along the meandering streets were skinny poles that held up wires that branched into some of the buildings, and in the late afternoon, as the sun disappeared behind the hills to the west, electric lights appeared in some of the windows. There were people, both men and women, walking along the streets because there were no sidewalks, angling toward one or the other of the buildings that were alive with recorded music and dimmed lights, some of them colored neon that boasted American-made beers.

There were only a few other cars traveling the streets. Most of them were old Chevys and Fords that were of indistinguishable colors and had seen better days. Parked near some of the buildings were a couple of the cars, but most of the people were getting along on foot.

When it was finally dark, Tynan turned around, back toward the better sections of the town, found a place where there were several cars parked, and abandoned his to the fates. On foot, he headed back to the poor people's bars. He noticed that the type of crowds had changed. Rather than looking like poor people returning from their jobs in the city, low-paying jobs that provided enough money for food and shelter and little else, these were the people of the night. The women wore amazingly short skirts and tight, revealing blouses, and they smoked in public and hawked their wares almost like the owners of the small craft shops. The men were dressed in jeans and shirts, all clean but ragged and frayed. They too smoked, the cigarettes dangling from their lips, and a spare tucked behind an ear hidden by slicked-back, heavily Brylcreemed hair.

As he walked along, Tynan ignored most of it, aware that his newer clothes and nearly pasty white skin compared to that of the locals marked him. He could feel eyes on him as he invaded the territory of these people. He could feel their resentment of him and didn't understand all of it.

In front of him he saw a long low building that had a single light on the outside in an attempt to illuminate the street. Music, American rock, vibrated from it, and there was cheering inside. A lone neon sign advertised Coors beer in a single window.

As he approached, he noticed four men standing near one corner, almost as if they were taking the names of those who entered. They stood in a line, shoulder to shoulder, watching Tynan closely. Tynan stared back at them, and when none of them made a move toward him, he entered the bar.

His eyes were drawn to a rear corner where a spotlight that could have called Batman to the center of Gotham City was shining on a single woman who swayed in time to music that only she heard. The driving beat of the rock that was blaring from somewhere else had no bearing on her dancing. Tynan shouldered his way through the cheering men until he stood close to the miniscule stage.

The woman had long black hair tied into twin braids that gave her an Indian look. Her skin was extremely dark and glowed with a light coating of sweat. Her features were fine. She had small, almost oval-shaped eyes, a tiny nose, and a little mouth. Tynan was surprised at her coloring, a uniform dark mahogany. Even her nipples were dark. But then she reached down and began to roll her miniature bikini bottom lower. Slowly she revealed skin that was a light coffee-and-cream brown. She eased the panties along her thighs, revealing a patch of pubic hair that had been dyed a stark blond.

When the crowd saw that, they went wild, screaming and hollering for her to take it all off in a mixture of Spanish, English, and a dozen local Indian dialects. She obliged by bending at the waist, keeping her knees locked straight, and rolling the panties slowly to her ankles. She lifted one foot, freeing it, and then kicked the panties into the audience. There was a mad scramble for the garment that resulted in two fistfights. The woman paid no attention to it. She kept swaying to the unheard music.

With that Tynan turned and worked his way back to the bar, which was little more than a couple of two by twelves set on sawhorses. A burly man in a sweat-stained and dirty white shirt was handing out beer to anyone close at hand who held a couple of bills up for him to see. His black hair was thick with Bryl-creem and slicked straight back.

Tynan showed him an American dollar and was rewarded with a lukewarm beer in an almost clean glass. Tynan knew better than to try to order the Coors advertised in neon, or anything else. All he would get was whatever the man happened to grab.

He took an experimental sip and then turned to survey the rest of the bar. In the corner farthest from the dancing woman was a group of rough wooden tables. Twenty-five or thirty men were gathered around the tables, their heads close together as they shouted at one another over the music. They ignored everyone else. Scattered around, some standing by themselves, others huddled with men, were fifteen women. All were dressed basically the same way in tight, revealing clothes. While Tynan watched, a man, his hand down the blouse of one of the woman and massaging her chest, was led from the room, toward the rear where there was a dimly lit staircase.

Tynan was drinking from his beer when a woman touched his arm and asked in fair English, "Say, gringo, you want to maybe go up the stair with Louisa? Huh?"

She was a pretty woman with but one flaw, a thin white knife scar that crossed her black eyebrow and cheek. Her black hair was pulled back in a ponytail that reached nearly to the floor. There was sweat beaded on her forehead, on her upper lip, and between her breasts.

"'Fraid not, Louisa," said Tynan.

"Hey! Gringo, I am not Louisa. She's over there," she said, pointing.

"Sorry. It's still no."

"Hokay! You be sorry that you don't want Louisa. She a real beautiful person. She give you the ride of your life. Bouncy bounce."

The large man who had been standing next to Tynan turned as the woman left. In a voice that failed to disguise its hostility, he hissed, "What is the matter, gringo? You don't like our women? You think they maybe got the disease?"

Tynan finished his beer and set the bottle on the bar. "No, I think your women are lovely."

"Then what is your problem?"

"No problem. I just came in for a drink. That's all," said Tynan.

"Why did you come in here where you are not welcome?" asked the man.

"To ask a question. A simple question. I was wondering if anyone in here has ever heard of the Light on the Trail."

It was like someone had thrown a switch around them. The talk and laughter and challenges ceased. Every eye was on them, every head turned toward them.

"You better get out of here," said the man. "You are not welcome here."

Tynan looked from the man's face to those surrounding him. Each seemed to be waiting for him to say or do something. Tynan smiled and said, "Yes. I guess I better leave. I see what you mean." He took a step forward and waited for the men there to move out of his way.

"And do not come back, gringo."

Two of the men moved back, out of his way. Tynan then saw a path slowly clear to the door. Out of the corner of his eye he caught a flash of light on metal. He spun to the right and waited. The man moved, his arm streaking upward. Tynan sidestepped and caught the man's forearm with his hand, the point of the knife inches from his belly. Tynan grinned at his attacker and twisted the arm slowly, feeling the man shift his weight to resist. Tynan locked his eyes with those of the assailant and when he had the man's attention, Tynan stomped on the top of the enemy's foot.

There was a shriek of pain and the man forgot about his arm being held. Tynan twisted it to the outside and then brought his knee upward quickly, hitting him in the elbow, straightening the arm with a snapping of bone. The man's eyes rolled in pain and he dropped his knife. Tynan shoved him backward, off balance, and he staggered into the crowd.

For an instant no one moved. There was the sound of shouting from the men watching the naked woman dancing and the pounding beat of the rock music, but around them, it was silent. Tynan watched the assailant for a moment but he didn't move. He was held upright by two of his friends, all of them staring at Tynan. Tynan reached the door without any trouble. He turned and looked back, but the angry men were returning to the bar, to the beer, and to the dancing woman.

Outside, he noticed that the four men had vanished from the corner of the bar. He didn't worry about it, hurrying across the hard-packed earth, into the shadows along the side of the road. He reached behind his back and felt the comforting weight of the Browning tucked into his waistband there.

''Hey, gringo!'' shouted a voice from behind him. ''Hey! You, gringo, wait for us. We want to talk.''

The last thing Tynan wanted to do was talk to four unidentified men on their home turf in the dark. He ignored the call and began walking rapidly for his car, which was a good mile distant.

''You stop now!'' came the voice.

But Tynan didn't stop at the command from the man. He reached around and slipped the pistol from his waistband and carefully transferred it to his front pocket, keeping it against his body so that the men chasing him wouldn't see it. With his thumb he removed the safety.

The voice came again, but this time it was much closer. The men had started to run, moving quietly along the side of the road.

Without warning, Tynan spun to face them. They stopped suddenly, four abreast, grinning at him. The single light from the bar was too far away to provide any illumination, but there was a nearly full moon overhead. In its cold light Tynan could see that two of the men were grinning, their teeth standing out in their faces almost like beacons, a hint of gold in their mouths.

"Hey! Gringo!" said one of the grinning men. "Why joo want to know about the Light on the Trail? Why joo come here asking your horseshit questions?"

"Do you know something about them?" asked Tynan conversationally. Slowly he eased his pistol from his pocket, trying to prevent the men from seeing the movement or the weapon.

"I think maybe joo are CIA. I think maybe joo are not going to leave here in one piece. I think maybe we cut joo up just a little for the lesson."

Tynan shrugged and smiled. "Why don't we just forget the whole thing." He understood why Wilson had not wanted to give him the weapon. He had been incountry just a little more than twelve hours and already he had been in one fight and was about to get into another. Of course, it would have still happened, even if he didn't have the pistol, but with it he could leave four dead men in the dust.

"Hey! I think maybe we teach joo a lesson for all your gringo friends."

At that moment, Tynan knew that there was no way that he was going to be able to talk his way out of trouble. The men in front of him were intent on cutting him. He saw one knife flash in the moonlight.

Tynan leaped close to the leader of the group, the grinning man who had spoken to him. Tynan brought his pistol up but didn't threaten the man with it. Instead he hit him across the bridge of the nose, hearing the bone crack with the impact. There was a spray of blood as the man collapsed to the dirt. Tynan kicked to the side as the man fell, hitting one of his friends in the side of the knee, snapping bone and tearing tendons and cartilage. That man screamed and dropped to his side, holding his knee in both hands.

Tynan spun and stuck the pistol into the face of the grinning man nearest to him. "You want to try something?" he hissed.

The man raised his hands, dropping the folding knife that he had held. He smiled wider and began backing away, chattering in Spanish so rapid that Tynan couldn't understand him. Suddenly he whirled and fled into the darkness.

The last of the attackers had backed away, but stood watching Tynan warily. His eyes flickered between the men on the ground and the American with the pistol.

Tynan began to retreat slowly, keeping his eyes on the wounded men. He didn't know if the men of South America had a code of maschismo like their Mexican counterparts, but if they did, they would have to repay him. They would have to come after him if they could find him. Tynan hurried from the area, keeping his eyes peeled, but reached his car without incident. He hoped that he had left no clues about his identity behind him, dropped during one of the fights. He unlocked his car door and yanked it open. After he was safely inside, he made sure that each of the doors was locked and then leaned forward, his head resting on the steering wheel, breathing deeply, as if he had run all the way back. The night had not been very successful.

6

While Tynan was just beginning his early afternoon drive through Quito, the rest of his team sat in their jeep outside one of the many PX-run snack bars, eating the sandwiches they had just bought and soaking up the tropical sun. Sterne, who had one foot up on the dashboard and one elbow on his knee, said, "I don't know what the skipper wants us to do about weapons. We can get all we need from any of the armories here, especially if the general authorizes it."

Boone shook his Coke and listened to the ice rattle in the paper cup. "The skipper said for us to arrange weapons, so we have to arrange it."

"But what weapons? What are we going to need? M-79s and LAWs or just a couple of M-16s and a pistol apiece? And how is he going to smuggle them into Ecuador anyway?"

In the back, Jones pulled the top off his Coke and used his straw to stir the ice. He took a deep drink and said, "This whole thing leaves a lot to be desired, just as the provost marshal told us. Hell, we don't have any idea what we're supposed to be doing."

"You know," said Boone, "we could probably make a phone call and accomplish everything we need to accomplish. Find some NCO who is in charge of an armory and tell him what we need. He could tell us whether they had it or not and who we needed to coordinate with. We then would have the afternoon free to screw around.''

"To do what?" asked Sterne.

"Fuck! Whatever we want to do, dummy," said Boone. "There's no way we're going to get the weapons today anyway. Besides, if we did get them, what would we do with them? We can't leave them lying around the room. Now there's a couple of swimming pools around here for us too. We could go into town and gamble if we want. Whatever.''

"The skipper said we should arrange for the weapons," said Jones.

"Right," agreed Sterne, "and we can do that on the phone. Boone's right about that. We can't really do anything until the skipper gets back to talk to the officers, and lets us know what the hell is going on.''

Boone dumped the ice out of his cup and then crushed it, dropping it to the floor of the jeep. "I'll let you guys off at your quarters and then I'll check around and see what I can learn.''

"I'd like a ride over to the NCO quarters at Howard," said Jones.

Sterne dropped his foot to the floorboard, turned in his seat, and asked, "There a reason you want to go hang around with the Air Force?''

"Yeah," responded Jones. "Jealous?"

"Mildly," said Sterne. "Just mildly.''

It was an hour after the fight that Tynan parked his car and then walked back to the International House Hotel in downtown Quito. The doorman let him in and Tynan was halfway across the lobby when he heard someone call his name. He stopped near a Victorian couch, two wingback chairs, one of which was occupied, and long low table, and searched for the feminine voice who had called him.

It took him only a second to spot Suzy Hamilton nearly running across the lobby. When she saw that he was waiting, she slowed and waved at him. "Hi, Mark."

"What are you doing here?" he asked.

"Waiting for you. I thought that you might want someone to show you around."

Tynan thought about the men in the bar, and those outside it, and the woman who had been dancing in the corner. "I've been around. I've seen all that I've needed to see around here. I thought I'd just head up to the room and sleep."

"Without buying me a drink first?" she said. "I've been waiting quite a while."

Tynan looked at her closely. She had changed from her work clothes into a light dress that came to midthigh and was cut low in the front. She had a white sweater wrapped around her shoulders to protect her from the late evening chill and the icy air that was being circulated by the hotel's air-conditioning system.

"You know," said Tynan, taking her hand, "sometimes I'm very slow on the uptake. I don't know what it is, I just am. Of course I'll buy you a drink. I could use one myself."

As they moved toward one of the many bars in the hotel, Tynan realized that he was playing a game where he didn't know any of the rules. The run-in with the locals had proven that. He had somehow antagonized them without meaning to, without knowing that he was. It could be that they just didn't like to see rich Norteamericanos, people who could afford the expensive rooms in out-of-reach hotels and could patronize expensive bars invading their home territory. Maybe they didn't like seeing people who paid more for a single suit than the locals could make in a year of back-breaking work ten or twelve hours a day. Or maybe it had been the question about the Light on the Trail. Maybe the locals felt an obligation to protect the terrorists, or lived in fear of them.

They reached a set of double wooden doors with an oval frosted window and a brightly polished brass handle in each one. Tynan held the door open for her and she stepped into the dimly lit interior of the bar. She moved to the rear, to a table that was shielded behind a giant hanging plant with leaves that nearly dragged on the floor.

Just as they sat down, a cocktail waitress in a costume that looked as if it had been modeled after the ones worn by the waitresses in the beer hall in Panama came by to take their orders. When she was gone, Hamilton leaned forward so that her hands were near the center of the table and asked, "What are you doing in Ecuador, Mark Tynan?"

He was about to give her the cover story that he had prepared, but then remembered she had been there when the Marine had given him the Browning. Although the package had been wrapped, it was fairly obvious what it was, and with that, she wouldn't be inclined to believe that he was on a sightseeing tour.

"Let me just say that it's a classified mission," he said, realizing just how melodramatic that sounded. It was the worst line from the worst movie.

"Okay." She nodded. "I understand. Is there anything I can do to help you?"

The waitress returned before Tynan could answer. She set down the drinks—a bourbon, neat, for

Tynan, and a daiquiri for Hamilton, on the table between them. When the waitress was gone, Tynan said, "You're going to accept that just like that. No questions. No nothing?"

She smiled. "You forget where I first saw you. There have been quite a few men who have come through there with missions they can't talk about. I'm used to it."

Suddenly warning bells sounded and red lights flashed in Tynan's head. He looked at her again, carefully, studying her in the subdued lighting of the hotel bar. Her brown hair looked natural enough. He could see no evidence it had been dyed, although if it had it would mean nothing. He looked into her eyes, and even in the dim light he could see that they were deep, dark blue. And if it hadn't been for Bobbi Harris, a woman Tynan had met in Vietnam, he might have thought that he had never seen eyes so blue.

He reached across the table and took her slender fingers in his hand. Her skin was smooth, almost silky, and there was no evidence of calluses on the tips. She hadn't worked on a farm or in the fields.

"Where are you from?" asked Tynan.

"Kentucky. Paducah. A little place on the Ohio River that's close to Illinois and Missouri. Born and raised right there."

"Paducah, Kentucky," he repeated. "I didn't know anyone was born there."

"One or two of us." She smiled. "Went to high school there and was a cheerleader, played some basketball on the girls' team, and studied at the community college to get a degree in business. So, what do you do?"

"I'm in the Navy," said Tynan noncommittally. He was trying to figure out why he was suspicious.

It was flattering that a good-looking woman would come to his hotel and wait for him to buy her a drink. Very flattering. And the more he thought about it, the less he liked it. He wondered if she had another motive, and suddenly realized that she worked for Wilson. The colonel had no idea what Tynan was doing in Ecuador and he wanted to know. The colonel had sent his attractive young secretary out to learn what Tynan was doing.

Of course, I could be wrong, he told himself. She could actually be interested in me. He smiled at the thought and didn't believe it for a moment. He was not so handsome or so rich that women threw themselves at him. The real test, he decided, was to see just how far she would let things go.

He drained his drink, saw that she had only finished half of hers, but said anyway, "Let's go up to my room. I'll have room service send up something more for us to drink."

She hesitated and then smiled coyly, licking her lips slowly. "You're trying to get me up to your room for ulterior motives."

Tynan rubbed a hand across his face and said, "No. I just need to go someplace where I won't be on public display." Tynan lowered his eyes and stared at a water spot on the table. "You don't have to come with me."

"Well," said Hamilton, "when you say it that way, how can I refuse?"

"Sorry," said Tynan. "I didn't mean it quite the way it sounded. I've been on the go since early this morning and I haven't had a great deal of luck today."

She slid across the bench behind the table, grabbed her purse, and stood up. "Let's go. I'm a big girl and can take care of myself."

They walked across the lobby to the elevators. Tynan punched the button for the elevator. As they stood waiting, she grabbed his hand, pressing her breast against his arm. They entered when the doors opened. She turned toward him, looking up into his eyes, but at the last second another man leaped between the closing doors.

"Just about missed it," he said.

"Almost," said Tynan.

They got off on the sixth floor and walked down the long hallway. He opened the door for her and she entered, nearly pulling him with her. As he kicked the door shut with his heel, she kissed him, forcing her tongue into his mouth, and pushing him back so that he was leaning against the door.

"Wow," she said, breaking away from him and kicking off her shoes.

Tynan stepped past her to the phone and dialed room service to request a bottle of bourbon, a bucket of ice, and a couple of mixers. He watched her move to the chair and sit down, crossing her legs slowly.

When he hung up, she said, "How's it been a bad day?"

"What?"

"Downstairs you said it had been a bad day. I wondered how it had been a bad day?"

"I believe," said Tynan, removing his jacket, "that I said I hadn't had a lot of luck today."

"Same thing. Tell me about it."

They were interrupted by a knock at the door. Tynan opened it and got the bottle, ice, and mixers from the bellboy, then set them on the combination desk-dresser-TV stand that dominated one wall and signed the check. He closed the door, turned and got two glasses from the bathroom. He picked up the ice chest and said, "You want ice?"

Hamilton stood and stopped him. "Don't bother. I don't need ice. Just give me a drink."

Tynan poured a couple of fingers into one of the glasses and handed it to her. "There you go."

She took a deep drink and stepped to the bed, sitting on the edge. She crossed her legs again and then hooked a foot on the railing of the bed. Her skirt slid up, revealing her thigh. She looked down and then back up at Tynan, smiling.

"Your bad day?" she prompted again, slurring her words slightly.

"It's not that important. It's over now, and tomorrow I think I'll just go back to Panama."

"What do you do in Panama?" she asked, and then drained her glass. She held it out like Oliver Twist asking for more.

Now Tynan felt he was on solid ground. "Training. I was taking a survival course there. Just running around the jungle trying not to get bitten by a poisonous snake." He reached for the bottle and poured her another shot.

She giggled and drank it down quickly. "I started before you arrived," she said, as if to explain her rapid plunge into inebriation. "Long before." She shrugged the sweater from her shoulders, uncrossed her legs, and leaned back. "Long before," she repeated. She rolled to her side and propped her head on her hand.

Tynan was amazed by the show. She had managed to arrange herself so that her skirt was nearly wrapped around her hips and her breasts were almost falling free from her blouse. "You had some trouble today," she cooed, trying to get him to talk about himself.

It was time to make his move, he decided. He stepped to the bed and leaned over to kiss her.

She rolled to her back, and had a hand behind his neck, pulling him to her. She held him tightly. With her free hand, she fumbled at his belt buckle. Suddenly she froze, broke the kiss, and put her hand to her forehead. "Oh, wow, I'm suddenly very dizzy."

Tynan watched as she struggled to sit up while tugging at the hem of her skirt. A soft moan escaped from her lips and she fell back, started to say something, and then seemed to lose consciousness.

Tynan wanted to applaud. It was a brilliant performance. She had remained conscious just long enough to straighten her clothes before she passed out. Tynan rolled to his right and stood. By leaning forward he could just see her left nipple because the fabric of her dress had bunched together. He doubted that she knew that.

Tynan picked up his drink, finished it, and set the glass on the dresser. He thought about peeling her out of her clothes so that she could sleep comfortably through the night, but decided that it just wasn't worth the effort, although it might be interesting to see if she had a plan to prevent it. Then he decided that she would let him do that, but if he tried anything else, she would stop it some way.

He sat in the chair and stared at her. She was a pretty woman. Her legs were very shapely and she managed to display them at every opportunity. He got to his feet finally, and rather than trying anything underhanded, Tynan flipped the bedspread across her, covering her from head to toe. That done, he turned off the light and felt his way to the bathroom so that he could brush his teeth.

Before he went back to the bedroom, he pulled out his wallet and checked it. There was his green military ID that proved he was a naval officer. There were various credit cards, pictures of friends including one of Bobbi Harris, a woman that Tynan sometimes thought he loved, a folded-up MPC certificate from the Philippines and dated during World War II, a library card, and a half dozen honorary memberships, including the Turtles. Nothing that would give away any secrets. He slipped it back into his hip pocket.

He stripped quickly and moved back into the bedroom. He crawled into the bed, trying not to shake it. He slipped his pistol under the pillow, rolled to his side, and went to sleep.

Long before morning, Tynan felt the bed shift slightly and was immediately awake. He didn't move as Hamilton eased herself from under the bedspread, obviously trying not to wake him. He watched her stand and first straighten her clothes, pulling her pantyhose taut and smoothing down her skirt.

She then turned toward him as if waiting for him to speak. When he didn't she searched the room quietly, efficiently, finding his wallet in his pants. She carried it into the bathroom and closed the door before turning on the light.

Still he had nothing that was proof. Maybe she was curious about him. He certainly hadn't given her anything definite. Maybe she just wanted to find out if he was married. Or maybe she thought she would find a microdot with secret instructions on it. He smiled at the thought.

In a couple of minutes she was done. She turned off the light, opened the door, and dropped Tynan's pants to the floor. She worked her way along the combination dresser-desk-TV stand to his suitcase. She opened it quietly, felt around in it, but apparently found nothing there that interested her. She closed it up, and then, rather than coming back to bed as he expected, she let herself out of the room.

As soon as he heard her close the door quietly, he rolled to his back and laced his fingers behind his head, staring at the dark ceiling. He watched patterns of lights from the cars on the streets far below dance in front of his eyes. He still didn't know what it meant, but couldn't see how it related to his present assignment.

In fact, the whole trip had been worthless. He had accomplished nothing, except identify himself to anyone in Quito who might be interested enough to notice him, although he didn't know why they would be. In the morning he would have to figure out a new plan of action because the one he had just wasn't working. He hoped that his men in Panama had come up with something when they visited the provost marshal. With that he rolled to his side and went to sleep.

The next morning Tynan checked both his wallet and suitcase carefully but nothing was missing. That was just what he had expected. Hamilton hadn't struck him as a common thief, and if she was, she wouldn't jeopardize her job by robbing someone who could identify her easily.

After showering, shaving, and brushing his teeth, he dropped his travel kit into the suitcase and closed it. He dressed in the same clothes he had worn the day before, checked the room to make sure he hadn't left anything or dropped anything, and went downstairs to check out.

He drove his car to the embassy, had a little trouble passing the Marine guard, but finally convinced the man that he was authorized inside. He parked, left the keys in the ignition, and went up to Wilson's office.

Suzy Hamilton was sitting at her desk. She had obviously gone home and changed her clothes, brushed her hair, and probably taken a shower. She was wearing a white blouse that buttoned to her throat. She looked up when she heard the door open and smiled. "Good morning, Mark."

"You look remarkable," he said, "considering that the last time I saw you, you were passed out."

She put a finger to her lips to silence him. "Don't say that around here," she cautioned him. "If Colonel Wilson heard you he would have me fired."

Tynan moved to her desk. "Why? What did you do that was so wrong?"

"Went out on the town and got drunk." She held up a hand to hold off his protest. "I know what you're going to say but it doesn't hold true here. We're in a foreign country and it doesn't look right for the embassy employees to go out on the town and get smashed."

"Okay, I won't say a word," he said. "How come you sneaked off though?"

"I had to get home and change. Some of us have jobs that demand we show up on time."

"You win," said Tynan. "Is the colonel in?"

"Yes, let me buzz him and tell him you're here." She put a hand on the phone and said, "You going to be around here tonight?"

"I don't think so," he said slowly, as if not sure about it. "I've got to get back into Panama."

"Oh." She picked up the phone and spoke into it. "You can go in," she told him.

Tynan entered Wilson's office and closed the door behind him. He drew the pistol from his waistband and set it on Wilson's desk. He added the spare ammo and then sat down in one of the wingback chairs.

"As you can see," said Tynan, "I didn't gun anyone down. All the ammo is there."

Wilson smiled coldly. "I have a report about a fight in one of the seedier parts of town last night. Several locals against a lone foreigner. You wouldn't know anything about that, now would you?"

"No, I don't think so," said Tynan. "Haven't a clue."

"I thought not," said Wilson. "What do you want this morning?"

"I'd like to get out of here. Back to Panama. As soon as possible."

"Just a moment," said Wilson. He opened a desk drawer and pulled out a folder. "Ah, this is your lucky day. We've got a military flight into Howard this morning. If you hurry you can make that."

Tynan stood. "I'll take that. I'll need a ride out to the airport and someone will have to turn in the rental car."

"I'll make the arrangements," said Wilson. "You hurry up and get downstairs." For a moment he was silent and then added, "I don't want to seem inhospitable but I'll be happier when you're out of here. I don't like hotshots blowing into town to do God knows what. They tend to fuck up international relations and then we spend six months or a year trying to patch up the damage they did without knowing it."

"Yes, well, thanks for all your help." Tynan turned and left.

He stopped in the outer office only long enough to say good-bye to Hamilton. She was nice enough, but there seemed to be an anger underlying her outer appearance, as if she wasn't used to failing to learn what she wanted. Tynan paused at the door long enough to take a last look at her, wondering if he wasn't reading too much into her attitude. In the light of day his sinister suspicions about her seemed unfounded. He shrugged, deciding that it really didn't matter now.

Downstairs he found a driver waiting for him. This time he didn't rate the limousine, just a normal staff car. Tynan rode in the front, spinning the dial on the radio, searching for an English-language station among all the Spanish.

At the airport he learned that he would be riding in the back of an Air Force C-130 that did not contain airline seats, but webbing and troop seats. The interior was not soundproofed. Tynan had ridden in the backs of C-130s a dozen times and didn't like it, but it would get him to Panama quickly.

7

On the plane ride back to Panama, insulated from
the crew and other passengers by the noise of the
four Allison T-56 turboprops, Tynan began jotting
down the notes from his trip into Ecuador. As he
wrote in the journal that he pulled from his suitcase,
tied to the deck of the C-130 between the two rows
of webbing that lined the length of the fuselage, he
realized just how flimsy everything sounded. He had
driven by the school where the abduction had taken
place but hadn't stopped and had asked no questions. He had driven around downtown Quito and
then to the outskirts where he had gotten into two
fights in five minutes but had learned nothing there
either. It seemed that he had just been looking for
an excuse to go to Ecuador and used the kidnapping
as it.

Tynan put the cap on his pen and leaned back,
his head resting against the red webbing of the para-
troop seats. He looked at the scribbled notes and
then closed his eyes. Once again he realized that he
was out of his element. He didn't know how to con-
duct a kidnapping investigation. Nothing had pre-
sented itself as he had hoped it would. Driving by
the school had provided no inspiration. Cruising the
back areas of Quito and checking the bars had provided no inspiration. In fact, Tynan wasn't even sure

what the next step should be. He hoped that his men had learned something from the MPs, but he doubted that they had. There seemed to be nothing to learn.

There was a sudden bump from air turbulence and a change in the sound of the engines, but everything settled down quickly and the loadmaster who was lying on the ramp in the back of the plane, a duffle bag for a pillow, didn't even move.

Tynan grinned at his own discomfort. He was sure that the plane was about to fall out of the sky, but none of the crew seemed concerned about it. He turned his attention back to his notes, reading what he had already written. There seemed to be nothing more to add. He closed his notebook slowly and then closed his eyes.

It seemed like it was only minutes later that the loadmaster was moving among the passengers, yelling over the engine noise that they would be landing soon and that they had to buckle their seatbelts. As he moved toward the front of the plane, he made sure that the passengers complied. There was a piercing whine from a couple of servos that signaled the landing gear was being lowered, and the ride seemed to roughen with the extra drag. Tynan thought that the plane was beginning to disintegrate. A few moments later, he felt the aircraft bounce once as they touched the runway at Howard Air Force Base in Panama.

They rolled up to a small terminal building, and the loadmaster opened the door on the left side of the fuselage so that the passengers could exit. Tynan was told that his suitcase would be available inside after it was searched by the customs agent.

As Tynan stepped to the tarmac, he was immediately hit by the tropical heat and humidity that was in sharp contrast to the dry, cool mountain air that he had experienced in Quito. He stopped long enough to wipe the sweat from his forehead and then turned at the sound of a horn. He saw Boone and Sterne sitting in a jeep behind a four-foot-high chainlink fence.

Tynan walked through a gate and waited as Boone drove up to him. As the jeep rolled to a stop, Tynan asked, "How'd you guys know that I was coming in now?"

"General told us. Called to make sure that one of us would be here to meet you and to let you know that he wants to see you the minute you get in."

"Yeah," Tynan nodded, "I thought he would be anxious to meet." Tynan walked around the rear of the jeep and looked at Sterne. "Why don't you climb into the back?"

"Sure, Skipper."

When he was seated, Tynan said, "Let's head on over to the general's office. Then one of you can come back here to collect my suitcase. As soon as I'm finished with the general, we'll have to meet."

"You think they're going to call this thing off?" asked Sterne, leaning almost into the front of the jeep.

"Let me ask you something," said Tynan. "Did you learn anything useful from the provost marshal?"

Boone turned the wheel and accelerated down the access road. He shook his head and said, "He said that without more to go on there wasn't much he could tell us. He wished us luck, but said that since we were dealing with a foreign country and foreign nationals and could control nothing, and since we weren't even working with the victim's family, that we wouldn't have much luck."

"Yeah," said Tynan, "that's kind of what I thought. I didn't have any luck in Quito except to learn that I really didn't know what I was doing."

"Then you think the general will let us get back to the survival school?"

"Don't be ridiculous," said Tynan. "Did either of you get coordinated with the armorer?"

"We can get whatever we want short of a 20mm antiaircraft cannon," said Sterne, "and if you really want one of those, I can probably work a deal to get you one."

They stopped outside the general's office building. Tynan got out of the jeep and said, "One of you had better wait here. I don't know how long I'll be. That doesn't mean that both of you have to stay. You can decide who has to wait and then drive the other back to his quarters after you get my suitcase out of hock in customs."

"Aye aye, Skipper."

Tynan trotted up the steps and stopped a moment to look at the deep green of the lawn that stretched for fifty feet to what looked like the edge of the jungle. Closer scrutiny showed that the jungle was a well-landscaped sea of tropical plants and trees. He took a deep breath of hot, humid air and then entered the outer office.

"Lieutenant Tynan, the general is waiting," said the master sergeant who had been horrified by Tynan's dirty clothes and muddy boots on their first meeting. This time he merely looked bored.

As before, the general didn't give Tynan a chance to report in a military fashion. He waved him into the office and pointed him to the conference area. "Have a seat," he said. "I'm sure that you remember Colonel Watters. Would you like a beer before we get started?"

Tynan walked across the hardwood floor, being careful because he was afraid of marring the highly polished surface. He sat down and said, "No thank you, General. It's a little early in the day for me."

"Well, not for me," said the general. He opened a bottle and then joined Tynan and Watters. "Now, what'd you learn?"

Tynan took out his notebook, glanced at the scribbled notes, and said, "I haven't had the time to prepare a formal report."

"That's fine," said the general, sipping at his beer. "I'm just interested in the highlights anyway."

"They'll be only a few of those," said Tynan. "I'm afraid that I learned next to nothing in Ecuador." With that Tynan launched into a detailed account of his last twenty-four hours, omitting only the session with Suzy Hamilton. He believed that neither the general nor Watters would want to hear about Wilson's attempts to learn his mission. He finished his report by telling of Wilson's hostile attitude that morning.

"So," said Watters, clapping his hands together. "The answer to our questions does not exist in Quito. What's your next move going to be?"

Tynan looked up, startled. "I don't have a next move planned. I assumed that someone who was better qualified would take over now."

"Your trip seems to have been a halfhearted effort, Lieutenant," said the general.

"Yes, sir, it might seem that way. But I don't know what else to do. I hoped by going to that bar, I might stir something up. I was successful, but not in the way I wanted to be. It seemed they resented my presence and didn't care about the questions I asked."

"Time is wasting," said the general. "You be back here at five for a briefing on everything we know. I'll put a call through to State and see if they might not have a little more information about the kidnapping and the Light on the Trail terrorists."

"Aye aye, sir."

"And you bring your team in with you. Be prepared to return to Ecuador, or to go where you must, by first light in the morning." The general stood and moved to his desk. He sat down, picked up a manila file folder, and said, "I'm getting tired of all this. State calling to demand that you, Tynan, go into the field to find this girl but not giving us anything to use. Hell, I can understand your problem. How do you start an investigation with no information other than someone is missing? There has to be more."

Tynan left then, went out, and got into the jeep with Boone. He waited for Boone to start the engine and back out of the parking lot before he said, "We have to find Sterne and Jones and be back by five. I'd like a chance to talk with you all before then."

It was thirty minutes later that they all assembled in Jones's room in the Air Force dormitory on Howard Air Force Base. Jones sat at the head of the bed, his back against the wall. Sterne sat Indian fashion at the foot and Boone sat on the floor. Tynan stood leaning against the wall, his arms folded.

"I wanted to tell you what I learned in Ecuador before we have to make the general's meeting at five. I should tell you up front that he plans to make us go through with the whole deal. State insists on it and so does he."

"Jesus," said Sterne.

"Sort of my reaction," said Tynan. "I had hoped that between talking to the provost marshal and my trip south to explore Ecuador that something would present itself. I'm afraid that it hasn't."

With that, Tynan spent the next twenty minutes repeating everything that he had told the general and Watters. When he finished he told them about Hamilton and her rather amateurish attempt to find out what he was doing in Ecuador so she could brief Wilson.

"Something strikes me as strange," said Boone when Tynan finished his report. "I don't like the way that Hamilton broad tried to horn in. Just stuck her nose in where it didn't belong. Something just isn't right about that."

"I know what you mean," agreed Tynan. "I figure it was just Wilson trying to stick his nose into my business."

"It's more than that, Skipper," said Boone. "It would seem to me that Wilson wouldn't have to go to such means to find out about you. All he had to do was pick up the phone and call the general here and ask."

"But the general would keep it under wraps for security reasons," said Sterne. "He wouldn't go blabbing to every swinging dick who gets a wild hair and calls."

"That's right," said Tynan, something stirring in the back of his mind. He snapped his fingers. "Of course." He pointed at Boone. "That's exactly it. If Wilson wanted to know something he would call the general and the general would tell him because Wilson would have both a need to know and the proper clearance. There was no reason for Hamilton to throw herself at me in her amateur spy attempt."

"Other than your magnetic personal charm?" asked Jones.

"If, for the sake of argument," said Boone, grinning, "we eliminate your personal charm, then why would Hamilton throw herself at you?"

"I think that we can safely assume that it was information that she was after," said Tynan. "I would be inclined to believe it was me if she hadn't so conveniently passed out and then searched my wallet the first chance she got."

"So," said Sterne, thinking as he spoke, "you did come up with a lead after all. Maybe not quite the one you expected, but a lead nonetheless."

Tynan rubbed his chin as he thought. Finally he said, "I doubt that she is going to lead us to the terrorists. That just doesn't make sense."

"Pardon me, Skipper," responded Sterne, "but I don't believe in coincidences. You go down to Ecuador to check on the terrorists and this lady searches your room. I would think that we would want to explore that more fully. If everything was above board, she could have asked Wilson, but she didn't. And if everything was above board, and Wilson told her to mind her own business, she would have."

"That means," said Boone, taking over, "that when we get back to Ecuador, you're going to have to meet with the lady and see what you can learn from her."

Tynan shook his head as if disagreeing but said, "What an assignment. I have to meet with a fairly attractive young lady to complete my mission."

"If you need any help with that, Skipper," said Jones, pointing to himself as if volunteering for a dangerous assignment behind enemy lines.

"I probably will," said Tynan. "I'll want one of you around she doesn't know so that you can follow her, if we get to that point."

"It would seem to me—" started Sterne.

Tynan held up a hand to stop him. "Listen, we have just enough time to get over to the briefing. They may have something new that makes all this speculation obsolete. Let's put it on the back burner until we see what the general has to tell us."

The general held his briefing in the conference area of his office, with Sterne, Boone, and Jones sitting on the couch, Tynan sitting on one of the chairs, and the general seated behind his massive desk. The briefing officer, an Army major who wore khakis that had been heavily starched and boots that had been spit shined, stood near the corner of the room where he could easily address either General McKibben or Tynan's men. He was a short, stocky man with black, wavy hair and a neat, trim mustache. He had three rows of campaign and service ribbons, but nothing that suggested a combat assignment or Vietnam service.

"The general and Colonel Watters," he said by way of introduction, "asked me to prepare this briefing with an eye on the activities of the Light on the Trail terrorist organization. My name is Major Pitts and this briefing is classified as secret."

He waited for a moment to let his words sink in, and then began a detailed briefing about the Light on the Trail, starting with its beginnings in the late fifties, talking about the known leadership and how they had all received scholarships to the university just outside of Moscow which was a front for the training of terrorists and counterinsurgents. At first they had no success, just a bunch of dirty and disillusioned kids from the richest South American homes who blow up high-tension towers, rural bridges, and empty airline offices. Only recently had they changed tactics, ambushing government vehicles and killing politicians.

"This latest activity," said Pitts, "is the first real attempt they have made at gaining any kind of international recognition, and we have to assume that it is all that it is. Just an attempt to get some headlines in the United States and western Europe. They have no real chance of forcing Vasquez y Sanchez to resign or to free any of the so-called political prisoners."

"This is all fascinating," said Tynan, interrupting Pitts, "but I don't see what relevance it has to our problem."

"The Light on the Trail has taken credit for the kidnapping and has made several threats against Sanchez."

"We already know that," said Tynan.

"Yes, well," said Pitts, "the difference is that we have now confirmed their involvement. Sources that I'm not at liberty to discuss here have informed us that the generalissimo has received some very explicit photos of his daughter, proving that she is being held by them. They also reveal that the terrorists are probably still in the vicinity of Quito."

"Can you narrow down the search area somewhat for us?" asked Tynan.

"First, let me say that the man killed in the ambush has been identified and we were able to locate his village. We are in the process of getting a man into the area to see what he can learn."

Pitts flipped the page of his report and got out a map. He folded it and looked for a place to set it. Finally he propped it against the side of Tynan's chair and pointed to it. "There have been reports of Light on the Trail activity in the mountains here. A large number of armed men, equipped with AK-47s, SKSs and Soviet-made rucksacks and other equipment. We can place them in certain areas and moving in certain directions, but we haven't uncovered their destination yet."

"Can we get that marked on the charts?" asked Tynan. "And taking it a step further, do we have any information about where their camps might be?"

"The military in Ecuador is already taking care of that problem," said Pitts.

"Anything else?" asked the general.

Tynan shook his head. "We just need Major Pitts to show us where the Light on the Trail operates."

"He'll take care of it," said the general. He looked pointedly at Pitts. "If you have nothing else to tell us, you may go. Please have the maps ready for Lieutenant Tynan as soon as possible."

Pitts looked like he was going to protest the breach of military regulations, but then simply shrugged. "Yes, sir. Within the half hour."

When Pitts left, the general said, "How soon can you get back into Ecuador?"

At first Tynan just shook his head. His mind raced as he tried to piece things together. He still didn't have a plan that would give him even half a chance to succeed. After talking to his men and listening to Pitts he felt a little more confident about the mission. At least he now had some ideas. Not very good ideas, but ideas nonetheless.

Before answering the general's question, Tynan looked at Sterne. "Weapons?"

"All we need is the general's authorization and we can have anything you want."

"How about getting them into Ecuador then?" Tynan asked Sterne.

"More of a problem there," said Boone, taking over. "We think we can get everything into a diplomatic pouch, but once we do that, we lose control of the weapons until they arrive in Ecuador. Someone else in the embassy will have to be the addressee. It might take three days."

"That's totally unacceptable," said Tynan. He was thinking of Suzy Hamilton, who would surely learn of the weapons if he was forced to use diplomatic sources, and that was something he wanted to prevent until he learned just who she was and whom she was working for.

The general stood and moved closer to them. "Are your men jump qualified, Lieutenant?"

"Yes, sir."

"Then I have a suggestion. We have access to Air Force C-130s and they are cleared for diplomatic overflight of Ecuador, or rather we can get them cleared. If you and your men parachuted in, you could carry any equipment you might want with you."

"I don't know, General," said Tynan. "There are things that need to be done. I've got to make contact with people in the embassy, so I can't enter the country illegally. We're going to need some local help."

"Dan'l and I can jump in with the equipment, Skipper," said Sterne. "Put us down somewhere near Quito and then someone else can drive out and get us."

"I don't know," said Tynan again. "I don't like splitting up like this at the last minute."

"That shouldn't be a real problem since you can rendezvous before you have to make a move. I'll get the clearances arranged and the flights scheduled,'' said the general. He picked up the map that Pitts had left on the floor by Tynan's foot. He scanned it and said, ''Looks like there are several good DZs close to the city.''

Tynan got up and looked at the map. He could see all kinds of problems, but then, there were a number of large open areas close to good roads. He said, almost as if talking to himself, ''This is going to take a lot of coordination. An awful lot of co-ordination.''

''I think we can get it done,'' said the general. He grinned. ''I find that I can get a lot of stuff done when I try.''

8

The man dressed in ill-fitting, patched pants and a frayed, faded cotton shirt, and concealed in a grove of pine trees, watched as fourteen men wearing sweat-stained camouflage fatigues and carrying Soviet-made AK-47s and SKSs worked their way along the narrow winding path. They stopped near a break in the split-rail fence that couldn't really be called a gate and used a five-cell flashlight to signal the hut. For a moment there was no answer, and then in the darkened window came a coded response. The men filtered through the gate and approached the door.

The leader of the group stopped short and, without speaking, pointed to several places around the hut, places that provided concealment and good fields of fire. Slowly his group dispersed, taking the positions and sinking into the shadows and cover until they were nearly invisible. Three of the men then entered the hut.

Inside there were two men playing cards at the rough wooden table. A third man sat in a chair in the corner and a fourth came out of the bedroom. He nodded to the three newcomers and then waved them to the chairs without realizing that there weren't enough.

The leader put his foot on the seat of the unoccupied chair and said, "Where's the girl?"

"In there," said the man from the bedroom, hitchhiking a thumb over his shoulder toward the closet.

"Get her."

The man moved from the bedroom door to the closet. He opened it and reached down, untying the rope that wound around her neck, holding her knees close to her chest. He grabbed her under the arms and jerked her out of the closet, forcing her to her feet. Then he had to hold her up as her muscles protested the sudden movement and she moaned quietly.

The new man inspected her carefully. Her hair was dirty and matted. There were fading bruises on her face, one eye was blackened, and there was dried blood from her nose on her chin. Bruises covered her chest and stomach and thighs. Her skin was filthy, as were her feet and hands. Her arms from the elbows down, where a rope drew them together, were discolored, as were her feet and calves.

"Clean her up," said the man, wrinkling his nose as her odor drifted to him in the confined cabin. "She's foul. Clean her up so that our fun isn't spoiled."

The man supporting her pulled his knife from his belt and cut the ropes around her ankles and knees and then pushed her savagely toward the door. She stumbled and fell but didn't try to get up.

When the man and girl disappeared outside, the leader of the men smiled and said, "We'll have some fun with her when she is more presentable."

A few minutes later there was a shriek from outside as the blood began to circulate into limbs that had been too tightly tied. There was a moment of silence and then another scream. The men in the cabin began to laugh as the sound of the pain drifted to them.

Fifteen minutes later Juana Gutierrez was shoved through the door to stand naked in front of her captors. The man who had just arrived stepped to her and stared at her face, but she kept her eyes on the floor. He grabbed her chin, forcing her to look at him, but there was nothing behind the eyes. She didn't speak or scream.

He smiled at her and slapped her once, and as her face darkened with the man's handprint, she still wouldn't look at him and refused to cry. He grabbed her hair, jerked her toward the bedroom, and pushed her to the bed. She landed on her chest and bounced, but didn't move. Her hands were still bound behind her.

For nearly a full minute he stared at her naked body. Then he stepped close and rubbed a hand over her bottom, exploring her carefully, but she failed to react. He grabbed her ankles and yanked her legs apart, studying her closely. Using the rope that had bound her ankles and knees, he tied one of her feet to the post at the end of the bed and the other to the frame, jerking the ropes painfully tight. He walked around the bed and took the rope that was still looped around her neck and tied it to the bed frame so that she was lying crossways, her legs spread wide and held fast.

Now he laughed, chuckling deep in his throat. "You know what comes next don't you? I'll bet you do," he said kindly, as if talking to his lover. "I'll just bet that you have it all figured out, don't you?"

He moved back so that he was standing between her feet. Roughly he reached down, rubbing her intimately, finally forcing his fingers into her. He continued to laugh as she failed to move.

At the first rough probing, she began to whimper. The pain was nothing like that she had had to endure the first few days while the men beat her with their fists and then with the wooden dowels. This pain was localized and no worse than a bee sting at first. But she began to cry as she realized what it meant. The psychological damage was going to be far worse than the physical damage from the beatings.

"When we're done," whispered the man, "we might decide to send your father one of your fingers to let him know we're serious. Wouldn't that be nice?" Don't you think he would be pleased with such a gift?" He then unbuckled his pants and let them fall to his knees. He crawled up on the bed between her outstretched legs, holding himself and guiding himself until he heard her cry out in pain, frustration, and rage.

It hadn't been dark all that long when Boone, Sterne, and Tynan crossed the tarmac that was still sun-warm, walking toward the C-130 parked there. When they got close, Tynan saw that the tail number was wrong and they altered their path, heading toward another Hercules.

"You sure you have everything we're going to need?" asked Tynan.

"Yes, Skipper," said Boone. "I checked the equipment containers, and the Army put in everything we requested. Their riggers got the pods set up and the chutes should open. You'll have to trust us on this."

"I trust you," said Tynan. "It's these Army guys I don't trust."

"Hey," laughed Sterne, "the one guy was a master sergeant and a master rigger and said that he'd been doing this since World War II. Did it in Korea and in Vietnam too. I figure that the chute will open right up. And they let us look into the pods. Everything we wanted and told the general to get for us was in there. Everything.''

"You guys understand what I want."

"Yes, Skipper," said Boone. "We have the DZ marked on our maps and we'll show it to the aircraft commander. He has been instructed to put us out where we want out. We collect the equipment pods and head to the road, keeping to the cover and wait for either you or Jones to show with transportation." He sounded exasperated.

"Sorry," said Tynan. "It's just that this whole thing has been thrown together so quickly with so many people adding their two cents' worth that I get a little worried about it."

"Dan'l and I'll have time to review all this on the plane, Skipper. We don't go out until first light. We'll check everything out one last time."

A large blue van loomed out of the half light on the ramp area, speeding by them. It looked more like a bread truck than a crew bus, but Tynan knew the flight crew was in the back of it. It pulled up to one of the C-130s and stopped. The rear opened and the Air Force people boiled out the back.

They caught up to the van and one of the Air Force pilots asked, "You the guys we're flying in?"

"Those two," said Tynan, pointing toward Boone and Sterne, who stood near him.

"Climb aboard. Where's your gear?" asked the loadmaster.

"Deuce and a half will be along in a couple of minutes with it. Somebody at the customs shop had to check it for drugs."

"Yeah," agreed the pilot, "we sure as hell don't want to smuggle drugs into South America."

The engine of the van revved a couple of times. Tynan stuck his head in the side door and looked at the driver. She was a two-striper dressed in fatigues, and it seemed that the tropical weather wasn't bothering her.

"Can you give me a lift back toward the BOQ?"

"Yes, sir," she said.

Tynan turned and said, "Good luck. I'll see you tomorrow sometime before noon if everything goes as planned."

"Aye aye, sir," said Boone. "Tomorrow."

Tynan climbed into the van and nodded. The driver slipped it into gear and they roared off, passing the deuce and a half as it drove toward the plane.

"Here comes the equipment," said Sterne, staring into the oncoming headlights.

It took them almost no time to get the equipment loaded and stored, the loadmaster strapping it down so that it wouldn't shift during the flight. That done, both Sterne and Boone sat down and buckled in, waiting for takeoff while the flight crew ran through their checklists and preflight procedures. Finally they were rolling down the runway and lifting into the warm night sky.

They had been airborne for about an hour when the navigator left the flight deck. He sat down next to Boone and leaned close to him to yell over the sound of the engines. "I want to check this DZ with you. Make sure that we're talking about the same place."

Boone nodded and pulled out the map he had tucked into the thigh pocket of his fatigues. He unfolded it and then refolded it so that Quito was near the top and the DZ near the center. He pointed to the area where he wanted to touch down.

The navigator took the map, studied it, and cross-checked it with his own larger scale map. He examined the relationship of the roads, fields, rivers, mountains, and towns and other landmarks, until he was sure that he had it positively identified. He plotted it carefully on his chart and then figured the direction from the TACAN near Quito. He nodded and smiled and handed the map back to Boone.

"That should do it," he shouted.

"How long before we get there?"

"If we go straight in, you'll have to jump in the dark. We're going to stand off the coast a ways and try to time it so that you have to jump just as the sun comes up to give you some light."

The navigator got to his feet, staggered once as the plane vibrated, and twisted his foot on the rails lining the deck. He steadied himself and disappeared up into the cockpit.

For a moment Boone studied his map and then tucked it back into his pocket. He unbuttoned his fatigue jacket, warm in the dual set of clothes he wore. Once they were on the ground, both he and Sterne would shed the uniform in favor of the blue jeans and cotton shirts they wore underneath. It was an old spy trick. Wear a couple of layers of clothes and as one got dirty, peel it off to a clean layer.

Boone propped his feet up on some of the equipment stored in the center of the plane and closed his eyes. He let the feelings wash over him, the vibrating of the plane, the cold air from the vent overhead somewhere and the heat from the floor. Cold on top and warm on the bottom. He didn't care. He ignored the subdued light and went to sleep.

Sterne woke him near dawn. They stood and moved to the back of the plane to use the urinal there. Then they began to put on the parachutes that the master rigger in Panama had given them. They checked each other, making sure that everything was fastened properly. Then they went over the equipment pods one last time to make sure that everything in them was secure and wouldn't be damaged during the bailout.

That done, there was nothing else to do but wait. Boone glanced at Sterne and saw that he was sweating heavily and rubbing the palms of his hands against his thighs. Boone leaned next to his ear and shouted, ''Nervous?''

For a moment, Sterne didn't answer. Then he smiled uneasily and shouted back, ''Yeah I'm nervous. I hate jumping out of a perfectly good airplane.''

''How many jumps have you made?''

''Sixty-two.''

Boone looked at him and then burst into laughter. ''Oh, a neo then. Will I have to push you?''

''No, I can handle it myself.''

The loadmaster approached them and shouted, ''About five minutes.'' He moved to the rear and opened the troop door, pulling it in and then pushing it up, out of the way. He then moved over to where the equipment pods were strapped down and freed them, jockeying them into position near the door.

When they were two minutes out, the loadmaster slapped Boone on the shoulder and yelled over the howl of the wind and the roar of the engines, ''Get ready.''

The jump lights next to the troop door glowed red. Boone moved closer, wrestling one of the equipment pods into position. Behind him Sterne did the same thing. Both had their attention on the tiny red light.

Just below him he could see the ground, dusky in the half light of the oncoming dawn. There was only an occasional artificial light, and Boone didn't know if it was electric or a farmer's lantern. In the States, on night or early morning jumps, he had been amazed at the sea of light below him. Hundreds, thousands of lights, from cars on freeways, farms, gas stations that were islands of brightness in the dark, small towns that glowed dimly and cities that seemed to be beacons for the heavens.

The pitch of the engines changed but the light continued its steady red glow. The loadmaster stepped close and yelled over the roaring wind, "We're making a go-around. Nav wasn't sure that we hit the right place."

The plane banked to the left and began a climb. Boone stepped back, away from the door and the icy wind that was whipping around it. He grinned at Sterne and shrugged. Both men knew that a go-around in a combat situation could spell death for the paratroopers on board, but then this wasn't a combat situation.

Within minutes they were on approach again. Boone was back in the door, the equipment pod in front of him, the static line linked to the aircraft. The red light glowed, but then the pitch of the engines changed as the pilot slowed and the light suddenly burned green. Boone shoved the equipment out the door and then stepped into space, looking at the tail of the plane. There was a suddenly snap as his parachute opened and he glanced upward to make sure that it had deployed properly. To his right, just above him, he saw Sterne, little more than a dark shape against a brightening sky, his chute fully deployed. Sterne was oscillating slightly and was pulling at his risers, trying to stop the swinging.

Boone hit the ground moments later, rolled in a perfect PLF, and was on his feet again, jerking at the risers and struggling to collapse the chute. He ran forward, rolling up the risers and then the silk of the chute. He dropped it all to the ground and hit the quick-release mechanism on his chest. He shrugged his way free of the harness and then turned, searching for the equipment pods.

Behind him, he heard a noise and whirled to find Sterne standing there. He was watching something on the far horizon and pointed to it. "You think he saw us?"

Boone then saw a single farmer moving silently in the distance, a dim silhouette near the horizon. "Couldn't have helped but see us. A huge airplane roars overhead and two men jump out."

"You think he'll report it?" asked Sterne, watching the farmer as he crossed the ridge line and disappeared from sight.

"Report to who?" responded Boone. "He'll just figure that it is something that is none of his business and go work his fields. Might mention it to his family, or might just keep his mouth shut."

"You sure?" asked Sterne.

"Nope, not at all, but I figure it's a pretty good guess," said Boone. "Why don't you locate one of the pods and I'll get the other."

In no time they had pulled both pods along with their chutes into a small grove of trees. Boone popped the top of one and checked inside but there was no evidence of damage from the bailout. He unloaded it and then stuffed the chute into it. He peeled off his fatigues and threw them in on top.

Next he retrieved his own chute from the field and put it into the pod. Sterne did the same with his so that both of them were now wearing civilian clothes.

Boone took one of the soft satchels and opened it so that he could load the equipment into it. He took inventory a last time, though if they had left anything behind, he didn't know how they would replace it.

He sat down on the pod and pulled back the sleeve of his light-colored cotton shirt so that he could see the time on his cheap Timex. He glanced at Sterne and said, "I make it three, four hours before we have to start worrying about someone arriving to pick us up."

"Yeah." Sterne nodded. "Did you spot the road on your way down?"

"Didn't really think about it," he said. "When it gets fully light, we'll climb the hill and survey the countryside. As I said, we've got a lot of time before pickup." He moved from the pod to the ground, letting the pod support his back, and then closed his eyes, not worried about anything.

9

The commercial plane touched down at Quito's airport shortly before noon. Unlike the last time, there was no limousine waiting as Tynan and Jones cleared customs. Together, Tynan and Jones walked through the airport terminal building. Once outside they spotted a sedan that bore U.S. Embassy plates. Tynan approached the driver and learned that he had been sent to escort them back to the embassy. The driver, a local man hired to provide the taxi service, opened the trunk and let Jones toss the suitcases into the back, but didn't offer to help. Jones climbed into the backseat then and Tynan got into the front beside the driver.

This time they drove straight to the embassy, and the driver didn't explain the points of interest to them. The driver stopped in front of the door, and Tynan and Jones were taken inside by a Marine guard. The receptionist seated behind a delicate-looking antique table in the middle of a giant room told them that they were expected in Wilson's office.

"You better wait here," said Tynan before moving to the stairs that led to the second floor. "I don't want Hamilton to see what you look like since you may have to follow her. When I finish there, we'll both go see the local man."

"Aye aye, Skipper. You still going to play up to this Hamilton?"

"Yeah. I guess I will. I'll try to sound mysterious so that she'll have an additional reason for wanting to go out with me. Keep her intrigued."

Jones shrugged and walked over to one of the waiting rooms and picked up a fresh copy of *Newsweek* and sat down to read it. Tynan went up stairs, stopped outside the office door, and prepared himself. He opened it and stepped in.

Hamilton was busy typing and didn't look up right away. She waved a hand at him to tell him to wait a second and finished her work. She was wearing a light-colored blouse that contrasted nicely with her dark hair. She finally took the yellow pencil from between her teeth and looked up. "Well, Mark!" she said, surprised. "I thought you'd gone home."

"Yes, well, I did. But then I got to thinking about you sitting here, wasting away, and had to come back to make sure that you were okay."

"That's sweet." She beamed. "But I suppose it's really Colonel Wilson you want to see."

"He's my excuse for coming in here," said Tynan, moving closer to her desk.

She lowered her eyes and said, "I'll buzz him." She spoke into her phone and then told Tynan, "The colonel will see you." She hesitated for half a second and then added, "It's really nice that you could get back here. I'm glad to see you."

Tynan put his hand on the knob but before opening the door said, "Nice to see you too. When I'm through in here, we'll talk."

"Good," she said, smiling. "I'd like that very much. I really did miss you."

Tynan opened the door to the inner office, shot a final glance at Hamilton as if searching for encouragement, and stepped inside. As he closed the door he said, "This is just to let you know that I'm back."

"I see that," said Wilson without looking up from his work. "I was told that you were inbound. You would like a weapon, I suppose."

"No sir, not this time. In fact, I doubt that I'll have any reason to bother you again."

Wilson sat there for a moment, studying the younger man as if looking for something wrong with the way he was dressed or maybe with his attitude. Finally he said, "Don't get yourself into any trouble while you're here, Tynan. The embassy might find it difficult to respond immediately to your needs. Do you understand me?"

"Yeah," said Tynan. "I understand you perfectly. If I do have a problem, you'll be the last one I call."

"Good. Have a nice day."

In the outer office, Tynan stopped long enough to say, "I've got another meeting down the hall in about three minutes. Would you care to have dinner with me tonight?"

"I have a—" Hamilton started to say, but then stopped. "Yes, I would like that very much."

"Where should I call for you?"

She smiled and said, "Why don't I meet you at your hotel. That'll be the easiest for everyone."

"Good." Tynan nodded. "I'm at the International House again. Haven't checked in yet, but have a confirmed reservation."

"About eight?" she asked.

"Fine. See you then." He left and shut the door carefully and stood in the hall, counting silently. When he reached ten, he whipped the door open again.

Hamilton looked up, startled, the phone to her ear. Without saying a word, she hung it up slowly and then turned to face him fully.

"I just wanted to say that I would meet you in the lobby since I don't have a room number yet."

"Yes. Yes, that will be fine." She smiled then and added, "It's going to be hard to wait until eight." She sat back in her chair.

"I understand," responded Tynan. "See you at eight." He closed the door and leaned back on it, grinning. Not exactly proof positive, but her reaction had been completely wrong. If the call had been innocent, she would have told him to wait a moment. The fact that she hung up without speaking to the party on the other end meant that he had caught her in the act. The only thing he didn't know was what he had caught her in the act *of*. There were a couple of innocent reasons, meaning that they didn't involve spying or international espionage, for her to make a phone call. Breaking a date with another man was one of them. Telling one of her friends about the sudden appearance of Tynan was another.

He didn't have time to worry about it. He hurried downstairs to pick up Jones, and then the two of them went to the fourth floor. The halls up there were not as plush as they were lower in the building. There was carpeting on the floor, but it was old, stained and fading. The walls had been painted once, sometime in the distant past, but the color had faded so badly that Tynan wasn't sure that it had ever been blue. Scattered along the narrow hall were long skinny tables. One of them had a single lamp sitting in the middle of it. Tynan could see that it was unplugged and the shade was crooked. They came to a scarred and scratched wooden door that had a tarnished brass *4* on it. He opened it and found a postage stamp–sized office with a single miniature window streaming sunlight. A lone man sat at the tiny desk that was piled with papers and reports and files. He had dark black hair combed straight back. He had bushy eyebrows and a prominent nose and the high cheekbones that suggested some Indian blood, probably Inca, somewhere in his past. When he stood, Tynan saw that he was short, maybe five six or seven, but burly. He had a thick chest that suggested he was at home in the higher altitudes of Ecuador.

"Are you Arturo?" asked Tynan.

"Yes. And you are?"

"Mark Tynan. This is Thomas Jones. You should have received a message about us from the State Department."

"Yes. Come in and close the door. Sorry I can't offer you a seat, but as you can see, I have not the room for visitors. Rarely does anyone come up to see me."

"I understand," said Tynan. "Were you alerted as to what we wanted?"

"Yes. I spent the morning going over the files on the Light on the Trail. What did you want to know?" He gestured at a stack of manila folders on his desk.

Tynan glanced around the tiny office. Jones had slipped into the only available chair. Tynan leaned against the wall and folded his arms across his chest. "What's their current status and strength, and where do they meet?"

"They have been quite active recently, as you well know. Strength figures have been hard to gather, as you can imagine. We place it between fifty and two hundred active members, meaning the people they can count on. Sympathizers might run the number up to near a thousand, but most of them would not actively help.''

''Location?''

''Latest reports put a training camp in the mountains east of here. I haven't been able to pinpoint it but I can get us fairly close to it.''

''Why hasn't anyone tried to find it before now?'' asked Jones.

Arturo turned to look at him. ''Before now, no one really cared about them. They were a nuisance in the country, but did little here in Quito. No one really gave a shit about them. Now they've entered the big time, and I just don't have the resources to go out after them. Besides, it's not my job.''

''I don't know,'' said Tynan, ignoring the exchange. ''Would they take a kidnap victim to their training camp?''

''We're dealing with terrorists who have limited resources. They might be forced to do that. However, I do have some information that a squad-sized unit was moving through the mountains yesterday. No destination has been identified, but that might be something too.''

Tynan laughed. ''Yesterday at this time I didn't have squat about where to look and now I seem to have more places than I can possibly search.''

''But all the places are close together,'' said Arturo. ''We can look at them quickly.

''Do you have any men available?'' asked Tynan. ''Men trained to use weapons and stealth?''

''I know a few men who might be willing to help us, if the price is right.''

''How much money are you talking about?''

''A hundred dollars apiece for the mission. A bonus for those wounded and a bigger bonus for the family if the man is killed.''

Tynan rubbed his head as if he was getting a headache. "A hundred bucks apiece is a little stiff," he said.

"Not for what you ask," responded Arturo. "You want men you can trust. For anything less you get alley fighters who you can't trust and who might decide there is more money to be made by shooting you and stealing your money and guns and anything else you might have."

"I see your point." He nodded. "All right. A hundred bucks, plus the bonuses." Tynan looked at his watch and realized that he was late for the rendezvous with Boone and Sterne. He said, "See what you can do and I'll give you a call back. We'll probably want to move at first light tomorrow."

"I can be ready by midnight," said Arturo.

"Good. We'll be in touch." Tynan opened the door and looked back at Jones. "Let's get moving."

In the hallway, as they moved to the elevator, Jones said, "You don't have any money to pay for local talent. What are you going to do, use your Bank Americard?"

"We'll have to hope that General McKibben will authorize the expenditure after the fact."

"Yeah. Hope," said Jones.

They spent the next hour arranging for a car and checking into the hotel. That finished, they bought a road map, compared it to the aeronautical chart and the topographical maps to locate the rendezvous, and then drove out into the country. Not far past the outskirts of town the road disintegrated into a randomly paved highway that soon changed to gravel. They sped along, kicking up a huge plume of dust behind them. Since the car had no air conditioning, they had all the windows open, making it hard to talk, especially with the dust swirling in through the windows and coating everything in a light gray.

They came to a fork and Jones hit the brakes, sliding to the right, the rear end nearly catching the front. When they came to rest in the swirling cloud of gray dust from the gravel and brown dust from the dirt, Tynan said, "Take the south fork and slow it down a little. We should be close."

Less than ten minutes later they saw Boone loping across a field of short green grass, waving at them. Jones pulled off the road, discovered that the field was dry enough to support the weight of the car, and drove toward Boone.

When they got close, Tynan leaned out the window and yelled, "Hi, sailor. New in town?"

Boone ignored the question and jerked open the rear door of the car. He scrambled in and pointed out the windshield. "Left Sterne up there with the weapons."

Jones tapped the acelerator and the car lurched forward in a cloud of dirt and grass kicked up by the spinning of the rear tires. Close to the trees he slammed on the brakes and spun the wheel so that the car slid sideways, stopping five feet from the first of the trees.

"We're there," he said.

"Getting a little wild, aren't you?" said Tynan.

"Lighten up, Skipper. I don't get to drive this way at home. Too many cops and not enough open fields."

Tynan reached over and turned off the ignition before jerking the keys free. He opened his door, got out, and went around to unlock the trunk as

Sterne appeared, carrying a long narrow satchel that contained two or three of the M-16s.

Boone ran into the grove, grabbed more of the equipment, and tossed it into the truck. A final bundle was put on the floor in the back.

When everyone was in the car, Jones started the engine after receiving the keys from Tynan and took off again, swerving to miss rocks and leaving huge dark ruts in the field.

As they reached the road, Sterne leaned forward and yelled over the increasing roar from the wind, "You were a little late, Skipper."

"Couldn't be helped. Secured us some new information and some assistance."

Sterne smiled. "And the young lady?"

"Dinner at eight and if you're real nice, I'll let you see her when she comes to the hotel."

They spent the afternoon coordinating all the efforts. They checked with Arturo and learned that he had set up his eleven men to meet outside the embassy grounds around midnight. He had secured transport for them and then made an effort to locate the Light on the Trail's training camp. He thought that he had narrowed it down to five square kilometers. Tynan told him that he was sending one of his men over to pick up a map so that everyone would be clued about the location.

At six o'clock, Tynan and his men were sitting in the hotel room, sipping bourbon ordered from room service. The sun was pouring in the window, heating the room and washing out the light-colored wall, reflecting brightly. Boone got up to draw the blinds and then sat down again.

"Now what?" he said nervously. "We just sit here and do nothing?"

"What do you want to do?" asked Tynan. "Or what can you do? There is nothing to be done until midnight. So we just hang loose."

"At least you get to have a nice dinner," said Sterne.

"You two—" began Tynan and then stopped. "Actually all three of you can go to dinner, just pretend you don't know me. Jones, you'll have to follow Hamilton. If we, meaning you and me, get separated, I'll get her back here. You can pick her up then." Tynan checked his watch. "Okay, I'm assuming that she's going to try to stay with me as long as she can. At about ten I want one of you to call the room. That'll give me an excuse to throw her out without making her suspicious."

"A late night phone call like that will just make her more suspicious," said Boone.

"Yes," agreed Tynan, "but she won't suspect that we're on to her. It'll just give her something more intriguing to worry about."

Sterne drained his glass and set it on the floor near the bed. "And then we head up into the mountains to meet with Arturo and his people."

"Providing I don't learn something from Hamilton that will negate that mission," said Tynan.

"And assuming that she actually knows something about the Light on the Trail. She just might be working for Wilson after all."

Tynan waved a hand. "We've already discussed that. I think we can rule it out. Now, does anyone have anything else to bring up?" When no one spoke he said, "Okay, everyone out of here so I can take a shower, put on my suit to get ready for this hot date. Take your glasses with you but leave the bottle for me."

Hamilton was right on time. She entered the hotel wearing a short skirt and light blouse. She carried a blue jacket over her arm, and when she saw Tynan she waved at him. In three running steps she was next to him. She hesitated for a moment and then kissed him lightly and quickly.

As they embraced, Tynan glanced over her shoulder and saw Jones nod at him, indicating that he was ready. Tynan pulled back, holding on to her hands, and said, "Where do you want to eat?"

"The restaurant here is just fine," she said.

Tynan pulled away from her and looked across the lobby. "If you'd rather go out," he said, "that's fine with me."

"Why complicate it?" she said, tugging at him, pulling him toward the restaurant buried in the corner opposite them. "I like the food here."

"That's fine." He led her across the lobby to the covered entrance to the restaurant. They stopped inside the door, at the podium where a short man in an immaculate tuxedo stood reading the reservation list.

"Yes, sir," said the man.

"Table for two?"

"You have a reservation, Mr., ah . . .?"

"No. No, I don't, but since it is early we thought that you might be able to squeeze us in," said Tynan.

"I am truly sorry, sir, but we are solidly booked for the next two hours. Perhaps if you would care to wait in the bar something could be arranged."

Tynan smiled and reached into his pocket. He had seen this a hundred times in a hundred movies. Every leading man worth his salt had bribed the maitre d' at some time during his movie career. Trying to be inconspicuous, Tynan pulled a twenty from his pocket. He knew that he was being overly generous, but he didn't feel like screwing around with a waiter when there were important matters to attend to. Tynan held out his hand to be shook and said quietly, "Possibly something will come free a little sooner."

The maitre d' turned back to his reservation book and shot a glance at his hand, surprised at the size of the bribe. He smiled, pearly teeth flashing in the soft lighting provided by candles and recessed low-intensity lamps, and said, "Sir, forgive my haste. I see that I have a cancellation here. We will be able to seat you immediately if you will follow me, please."

When they were seated, after the maitre d' had assured them that they would have the best service, Hamilton smiled and asked, "How much did you give him?"

"A twenty."

"That is too much. He'll be expecting—"

Tynan waved her to silence. "Doesn't matter. I'm on an expense account," he lied. "Someone else is picking up the check."

"You shouldn't tell a girl that," she said, leaning forward, her elbows on the table. "You're supposed to be trying to impress her."

"I figured I could think of other ways to impress her," said Tynan. He stopped talking while a bus-boy put water on the table, a slice of lemon floating in each of the glasses. Tynan stared at it and said, "What the hell is this?"

"The water here is terrible and they think that putting lemon in it makes it easier to drink." She took a swallow and then asked, "Now, how are you going to impress me?"

Tynan reached across the small table and unbuttoned the top of her blouse so that he could see the swell of her breasts. He smiled when she didn't move except to bring her arms closer together to deepen her cleavage.

"Well," he said, "I was going to show you a couple of things after dinner."

"Yes," she said, lowering her eyes. The tip of her tongue touched her lips briefly, moistening them. "I imagine that you could show me a few things like that. But there must be more than just after-dinner passion."

For a moment Tynan thought about making it difficult by trying to switch the topic back to sex, but then remembered that there were things that he wanted to learn from her as well.

"Maybe my job would impress a young woman who was on her own for the first time. I'm not just Joe Tourist, you know."

She laughed and said, "No, I didn't think you were, but you have been so strangely secretive about your occupation that I thought it was classified information or something like that."

"I would have thought that you would have known all about it already," he said. He leaned close again, across the table, and lowered his voice. "I mean, you work in the embassy. You should have some idea."

"They don't tell me much about anything," she said. "I hear things and I know that you're considered to be an important person by someone there. What I mean is, they don't send limousines to the airport to meet just anyone."

"It was a sedan today, with a rather rude driver," said Tynan.

''But that was your own fault,'' she countered. ''You complained about all the attention that the limo and driver got you the last time.''

''I suppose so,'' he said.

Now she reached up to unfasten another button on her blouse and then sat back so that the top of the garment drew apart, showing him her smooth, tanned skin. He could see a line of white on the top of her breasts where her swimsuit covered her while she sunbathed.

''So what are you doing here in Ecuador, Mark Tynan?'' she asked huskily.

''I thought you would figure it out.'' He stopped talking and looked right into her eyes. ''I'm supposed to find Juana Gutierrez for her daddy, the generalissimo,'' he said quietly.

For just a moment there was a flash of triumph in her eyes as she finally confirmed what she had believed. ''Quite a task,'' she said.

''A damned impossible one,'' said Tynan. ''I'm not an investigator. I've made the motions down here, but haven't really learned anything about the kidnapping. Tomorrow I thought I might head deeper into the mountains and see if I can shake anything free that way.'' He snapped his fingers. ''Say, you wouldn't like to come along, would you?''

''I wish I could, but I can't. Really. I have to work.'' She glanced around the restaurant and said, ''You don't really want to eat do you? I don't. I have something else, something much more fun in mind.''

''I just wasted twenty bucks impressing the maitre d' for no good reason.''

"Look at it this way," she said, getting to her feet. "The fact that we didn't eat is going to impress him even more."

"Good point." Tynan shoved his chair back so he could rise. He took Hamilton's hand and led her from the restaurant, stopping long enough to tell the startled maitre d' that everything had been just fine.

Alone in the elevator, she leaned forward to kiss him, slipping her tongue deep into his mouth, probing as far as she could. Her hand dipped below his belt and then she struggled to force it inside his pants. She just touched him as the bell sounded signaling their arrival on his floor.

"God!" he said. "I'm not sure that I could have taken it much longer. Saved by the bell."

"Not for long," she said wickedly. "Not for long."

Tynan fumbled with the key at the door, finally got it, and pushed the door open. He let Hamilton in first and then grabbed two glasses. "I'll get some ice," he said, disappearing into the bathroom. He made two drinks, watering his and then realizing that it was too light. He added a little Coke to darken it and then wondered just how good it would be.

He stepped into the bedroom to find Hamilton waiting for him wearing only high-heeled shoes and skimpy black lace bikini panties that hid nothing. He stood there, a drink in each hand, and studied her nearly naked body.

It was a good body, he had to admit. She had the best legs he had ever seen. Thin and shapely, and as she moved, he could see the outline of the muscles as they rippled. Long, smooth thighs that were lightly tanned like the rest of her. She had a tiny waist and flat stomach. Her breasts pointed at him like lethal weapons, the nipples standing erect.

Slowly she turned so that he could see her back and her bottom.

He set the glasses on the dresser and moved to her, taking her in his arms, kissing her. She responded, holding him tightly, rubbing against him with enough force to generate electrical power.

They moved toward the bed. Hamilton sat down and reached up toward Tynan. She pulled him close and kissed him again, forcibly. He touched her breasts, squeezing the nipples, and she moaned deep in her throat. He let a hand slide lower, across the softness of her belly, to the waistband of her panties and beyond it. He felt her gently, realized that she was more than ready for him, and began to massage her.

"Oh yes," she gasped. "Just like that. Please. Just like that."

He kept at it, working his hand and fingers, listening to her. He felt her stiffen and relax and stiffen again and then shout out his name. "Now," she pleaded. "Do it now."

The jangling phone surprised him enough to make him jump. His free hand stabbed out, snatching it from the cradle. "What?" he demanded. "What?"

He heard the voice at the other end tell him that it was time. That they had to go. "Now?" he said, holding up his end of the conversation. "Right this minute?" he grunted in response and slammed the phone back.

He kissed her quickly and said, "I've got to go to the embassy right now. I'm sorry."

Hamilton seemed to fall back against the pillow, her breath ragged. She took three deep breaths and said, "Right now? This minute?"

"Yes. Sorry."

She reached down and tugged at her panties, pulling them up her thighs until they were snugly against her. "Right now?" she repeated.

"Yes."

She looked around the room as if trying to spot someone hiding in the shadows. She flipped a hand and said, "I could wait for you to get back."

Tynan stood and adjusted his clothes. "I don't know how long I'll be. I could call you as soon as I break free."

She sat up and swung her legs around so that her feet were on the floor. She gestured with both hands, tiny circles cutting through the air as if she didn't know what to say. "I don't believe this," she gasped.

"You going to be okay?" he asked.

"Just great," she snapped. "You got one hell of a technique there, friend. Thirty seconds longer and I would have been a hell of a lot better off." She stood and walked to her clothes. She slipped on her blouse and then turned back toward Tynan. "You mind if I use your bathroom?"

"Go right ahead."

As she disappeared into the other room, Tynan sat down and drank most of the undoctored drink in a single gulp. He rubbed a hand over his face and began to realize the state that she was being left in. He heard water running and assumed that she was using it to take the edge off. He swallowed the rest of the drink as she came back.

She pulled on her skirt, zipping it and then smoothing it over her hips. She stuck her stockings into her purse and said, "Please don't ever do this to me again."

"I hear that," said Tynan. "This isn't exactly easy on me either. I really am sorry."

She bent down and kissed him on the lips in a sisterly fashion. She straightened, took another deep breath, and laughed. "Give me a call when you're through. Please."

Tynan got up and escorted her to the door, his arm around her waist, feeling the motion of her bottom when he dropped his hand to cup her. "Don't worry about it," he said. "I'll call you as soon as I can."

At the door they kissed again, quickly, and she left. He closed the door and leaned back against it. "Christ! What I do for the country and the Navy," he said.

As Hamilton left the hotel, Jones followed. He watched her descend the four steps to the sidewalk, slip into the jacket she carried, and then turn to the north. She hurried along, glancing right and left periodically, but never seeming to look back. She crossed the street in the middle of the block, and Jones thought about following but decided that it would mark him too easily. A lone man in the middle of the street would be easy to spot. He watched her, following on his side of the street until she turned a corner and he lost sight of her.

He crossed the street and ran along the storefronts, keeping to the shadows. When he came to the corner, he peeked around and saw her well down the block. He straightened up, ran a hand through his hair as if to comb it, and then casually stepped out, walking unhurriedly along, studying the few windows that held displays.

For several blocks they kept up the game of cat and mouse. Finally she ducked into a side street and a moment later came roaring out in a car. She turned to the north, drove a block, and then the turn signal came on. She disappeared then as Jones searched wildly for a taxi, but none was visible. He ran to the corner where she had turned, and in the distance he could see the taillights of a car flash once as it braked and then fade in the distance. The only thing he could say for certain was that she disappeared heading east, near the outskirts of the city.

He turned and walked back along the street, suddenly wondering if he was being followed. It hadn't occurred to him that there might be someone behind him until then, but each time he spun around, he saw no one there. Finally, feeling foolish, he decided that no one was following him and he walked back to the hotel.

Upstairs he knocked on the door and Tynan let him in. He walked to one of the chairs and collapsed into it. "She got into her car and took off. Last I saw her, she was going east, out of the city."

Tynan, having had the time to recover in a cold shower that nearly froze him solid, rubbed his chin and laughed. "I guess this just shows us what amateurs we really are. Never thought about her getting into a car and driving away. Makes us look pretty dumb."

"It was a long shot at best," said Boone.

"Yes, but if we're going to follow up on something, we should do it right. The least we can do is think it all the way through. I guess it doesn't matter now. Okay, let's get our gear and get into the field."

They got to their feet and left the room. They took the elevator to the ground floor and walked out to the parking lot. Tynan opened the trunk to check the weapons and then tossed the keys across the roof of the car to Boone, who caught them with a clapping motion of his hands.

"I don't get to drive, huh?" said Jones.

"No," answered Sterne. "We decided that we wanted to arrive there in one piece."

They all got in with Tynan in the front using a flashlight to read the map. He called out directions to Boone. Seventy-five minutes later they came to a bridge and on the other side were three parked cars. There seemed to be no one around them, but Boone pulled off the road and stopped behind them, turning off the lights and the engine.

Tynan got out and stood there for a moment. Suddenly, out of the gloom near the bank of the river, he saw someone. "Arturo?" he whispered.

"Yes. We are ready," said Arturo.

Tynan turned and leaned down, speaking into the open window of the car. "Let's unass the vehicle and get ready to move out."

"Finally," said Sterne, "it's beginning to seem that we're about to accomplish something."

Tynan nodded his agreement, although he wasn't sure what they were about to accomplish. He watched his men pass out the weapons and form up. Arturo and one of his men took the point and moved off into the dark.

Yeah, thought Tynan. We're about to accomplish something this time.

10

The first thing that Tynan realized as they started up the winding mountain trail was that he was badly out of shape. Within a hundred yards he was breathing hard, trying to suck the air deep into his lungs so that he could walk another fifteen or twenty feet. Sweat blossomed on his forehead and he swiped at it with the sleeve of his denim jacket.

He looked at the trail. In the bright moonlight he could see that it was a well-worn path through the mountain meadow, leading upward, toward a ridge that was probably two, three hundred feet higher. Bushes were scattered about the field, and there was a finger of woods that crept over the ridge and reached down toward the road. Tynan didn't think he would live until he got to it.

The very first thing he was going to do when the mission was over was begin a program of rigorous physical exercise. There was no excuse for being so winded after walking just over a hundred yards. He was only carrying a single canteen, a couple of flash grenades that weighed less than a pound, his weapon—a lightweight M-16—and about two hundred rounds of ammunition. It wasn't like he had a hundred-pound rucksack on his back, and yet the air was whistling through his nostrils as he tried to keep from passing out.

And then it struck him. The problem wasn't that he was out of shape but that he was at ten thousand feet where the air was thinner. You couldn't move from sea level in the tropics to the mountains without there being a problem with adjusting. Arturo and his men were used to the altitude, but Tynan and his boys were not.

He caught up to Arturo and rasped, "You have to slow it down. My boys and I aren't used to this altitude. You'll lose us."

"But if we don't move rapidly, we will not be able to ambush the camp."

"We don't know if we'll find the camp and we don't know if there is anyone in it," said Tynan.

"I have good information," said Arturo. "We will find the terrorists."

"Just the same," panted Tynan, "you'll have to slow it down. We're not used to the rarefied atmosphere up here. I feel like my lungs are about to rupture."

Reluctantly Arturo nodded. "We will try to walk slower for you and your men."

Tynan was bent over slightly, the breath coming rapidly, rasping in his throat and burning his lungs. "Thanks a lot," he gasped.

Finally they reached the ridge line, but rather than descending on the other side, they moved to the military crest so that they wouldn't be silhouetted on the horizon, and followed the ridge to the east and then to the south. They dipped down into a slight valley, up to another ridge, and then along it as they continued their march to the south. They came to another ridge, crossed it, followed a path down into the shallow valley and back up, into the trees that were spreading out there. They rested in the trees for nearly twenty minutes and then were up and moving.

After another hour Tynan caught up to Arturo to suggest a rest break, but before he could speak they both heard a persistent buzzing, a tiny sound like an angry insect near the ear. Arturo held up a hand to stop the patrol so that he could listen.

"That sounds like a generator," said Tynan. "A gasoline-powered generator."

Arturo grinned and said, "You see. I have found the camp already. No farmer would have a generator, and if he did, he wouldn't let it operate all night." He waved his men to cover and watched them disappear into the dark, hiding near bushes, in depressions, and behind trees.

Together, Tynan and Arturo climbed the rest of the way up the path until they were on top of the ridge. They got down and crawled forward until they could look down on the huge valley that opened before them. The sound of the generator was louder, drifting toward them on a light breeze.

Tynan scanned the dark ground. His eyes were drawn to a couple of dim lamps burning on the far slope. He studied the ground there until he began to see things hidden by the night. There seemed to be a couple of small buildings and two or three vehicles parked near them. A long winding road, a lighter color than the surrounding fields, led from the compound to the floor of the valley and then into the distance in the east.

"That must be it," said Arturo, speaking in a normal tone of voice.

"You sure?" asked Tynan, lowering his voice.

Arturo shrugged, "I don't know for sure. But that place does not belong to the government and it does not belong to a farmer. No farmer could own three cars.''

''We don't know that it is the training camp for the terrorists,'' Tynan reminded him.

''No, but it is in the area where it was reported to be and it does not fit into the profile of a farmer. It is something that does not belong.''

''Well, the least we can do is make the effort to check it out.''

They crawled back, away from the top of the ridge. Arturo waved once and the men crowded around. Quietly Arturo explained the situation and what they had seen. Tynan suggested that they stick to the military crest of the hill, on the other side of the ridge. That way they should be nearly invisible and could keep an eye on the camp as they moved into positions to surround it.

Arturo took over again, telling them that they wanted to cut off the possibility that the terrorists would escape. To do that they would all operate individually, eight of the men taking positions on the outside of the camp while the rest of them swept through, forcing the terrorists into the open.

Arturo pointed and said, ''You, you, you, and you five over there will set up ambush points outside the camp. I will lead the sweep through with the others. Are there any questions?''

''You said ambush points. I take this to mean we kill anyone who tries to escape,'' asked one of his men in Spanish.

''We would prefer prisoners,'' said Arturo, his nod lost in the dark, ''but no one escapes. Clear?''

''Clear.''

''Let's get going,'' said Tynan, checking his watch. It was about an hour until sunup. They would have the night to hide their movements and the sun to help them as they began the sweep through the camp.

Arturo got to his feet and began a rapid climb up the slope, keeping to the cover provided by the bushes and trees, slipping into the edge of the finger of woods as he approached the crest. Once over the top of the hill, he descended fifteen or twenty feet before turning deep into the woods. After only a hundred meters, he exited and faced only open ground, mountain meadows, and plowed fields lined with split-rail fences. He kicked the top two rails free from their posts and crossed into one of the fields quickly. At the fence there he halted and turned to look back. He could see the dark shapes of the patrol strung out across the field, but if he hadn't known where they were he wouldn't have been able to see them.

They worked their way around the outer ring of hills, circling the camp almost as if the terrorist base was on the side of a bowl and they were moving along the rim. When they were to the northwest of the camp, Arturo broke two of his men off, sending them down the slope to find hiding places to the southwest and west of the enemy. When they were due north, he broke off another two with instructions to hide northwest and north. They continued on around, finally reaching a point southeast. Arturo had scattered more of his men on the east side so that only the south was empty. They descended to the valley floor so that they were due south of the buildings, nearly standing on the road. Arturo sent men east and west of there so that every exit was covered.

Arturo crouched down behind the rusting hulk of an old car, the sides of which had been riddled with bullets of a dozen different calibers. He peaked over the hood, studying the camp in the semilight of the predawn. He shot a glance at Tynan who was sitting near the rear of the vehicle, his eyes on the house that dominated the surrounding territory.

There were four buildings in front of them. One appeared to be a large farmhouse that was three stories tall and might contain fifteen rooms. There was an enclosed porch on the front and three or four steps that led from a dirt walkway to the front door. Fifty feet to the east was a barnlike structure that had a huge double door, and even in the half light they could see tracks left by heavy-duty trucks. Farther to the right was a small building that bristled with antennas—probably some kind of radio shack. There was a single window behind which a dim light glowed. The rumbling of the generator seemed to come from that direction, though they couldn't see it. Beyond that was a small square structure that was about six feet tall. It could have been a blockhouse that contained weapons. Or it could have been a cell that contained the prisoner, though it seemed to be unguarded. The three cars were parked by the house. They looked like normal sedans that had been well used.

Scattered around them were a wide variety of broken-down equipment and half walls that gave the impression of an obstacle course. Leap the wall, put some rounds into the car, jump the narrow ditch, and then hit the dirt before scrambling over the fence.

Around them there was no movement. Neither Tynan nor Arturo could see guards. There might have been someone behind one of the upper-story windows in the house, or concealed near the barn, but it wasn't obvious. Arturo left his position and moved to where Tynan crouched.

"Are you ready?"

Tynan took a last glance at the compound. He pointed to Boone and Sterne and said, "I want you to hit that small building. The one with all the antennas on it. We need to take that out first in case it is the radio room. We don't want them sending any messages to anyone. But we can't have any shooting because it might alert people in the house. You have to take it quietly."

"Do we destroy the equipment?" asked Boone.

"Don't get overzealous, but make sure that no one is going to use it to call for help."

"Aye aye, Skipper."

"And the rest of us hit the house," said Arturo.

"As soon as we see Boone and Sterne disappear inside the radio shack, yes," agreed Tynan. "One guy in back to watch the door there. The rest of us into the front."

They nodded their understanding. Tynan looked to the east, where the sky near the horizon was glowing bright red that disintegrated into light grays the higher it went, until it was still dark directly overhead. Tynan looked at his watch and held up five fingers and said, "Five minutes."

Boone and Sterne, crouched low, worked their way to the front of the car. Boone looked around, checked Sterne, and then leaped from cover, sprinting across the open ground toward the radio shack. Then Sterne was up and running a half second later.

As they moved, Tynan ran from the rear, toward the front of the house. Jones, who followed closely, suddenly veered to the left, around a bush, heading for the back to cover there. In thirty seconds, Tynan was lying in the dirt at the foot of the steps that led up into the house. Around him were the rest of the attackers, Arturo on the other side of the steps with his three men behind him.

Tynan got to his feet, felt the wood of the riser, and then put a foot on it, near the edge where there was a smaller chance of its squeaking. With his left hand he reached out to balance himself on the higher steps and then, crouching low, moved upward until he stood on the porch. He looked over his shoulder and saw Arturo on the steps and his men still on the ground.

Carefully, so that the hard leather of his boots didn't scrape on the wood of the porch, Tynan eased forward. He shifted his weight slowly, cautiously, waiting for the wood to creak or pop, but that didn't happen. It took him nearly two minutes to work his way across the ten feet of the porch. That done, he leaned against the wall of the house and grabbed the knob of the screen door. It twisted easily and Tynan pulled it open an inch or two.

A moment later Arturo crouched by the door and was reaching through the gap that Tynan had made so that he could open the main door. He grinned, his teeth nearly flashing in the growing light as the knob turned slowly. The terrorists had not bothered to lock the front door. Security was surprisingly lax.

Tynan looked over the railing on the porch and saw that Boone was near the door of the radio shack. Sterne stood directly in front of it as if he planned to kick in the door. Boone pointed at him and then grabbed his rifle in both hands, preparing to dive through. Sterne leaned back and with his boot kicked at the door near the knob. There was a shattering impact that echoed through the valley, but the door held. Sterne kicked it again and it flew open. Boone disappeared inside but there was no shooting.

As that happened, Tynan jerked the screen door wide with a protest of rusty hinges. Arturo jumped up and pushed on the front door. It flew back to smash against the wall. Arturo was through it, followed by two of his men. Tynan went through last, his weapon pointing up the stairs that were in front of them.

Somewhere on the second floor there was the sound of footsteps as if someone was running down a hallway. Tynan positioned himself on the fourth step up, looking back into the hallway above him.

From outside came a single burst of gunfire, four or five shots on full auto. It sounded like Boone or Sterne because it came from the direction of the radio shack.

A shape appeared over him and Tynan fired twice, the muzzle flashes bright in the dark house. There was a wet smack and a scream as the shape disappeared rapidly, running away. Tynan began to climb the steps, his back against the wall, sucking air through his clenched teeth, suddenly sweating heavily in the cool morning air.

Below him, from the main hallway that led into the house, he heard someone issue a hushed order. There was a splintering of wood as a door was kicked in and then a sustained burst of automatic weapons fire. Tynan could hear the bullets as they riddled the walls of the house, smashed into the furnishings, and shattered the windows.

He kept moving upward. He stopped on the landing, his eyes barely above the second floor. He could see that the hallway was empty and that there was a large window at the far end of it now glowing gray as the sun continued to rise. Light flashed under one of the doors, as if the room's occupant had turned on the light long enough to find a weapon.

Now Tynan wished that he had brought real grenades. They were the best way to clear rooms. Kick
in the door, toss in the grenade, and then dive in to
finish off the wounded. Of course, all that didn't
work when searching for a hostage. He didn't expect them to be holding her up there, but then he
couldn't be sure.

He reached the second floor and stopped by the
first door. He put an ear to the rough wood and listened for a moment but heard nothing. Standing to
one side, he kicked in the door and tossed in a flash
grenade and leaped back, out of the way, his eyes
closed.

There was a burst of fire from the room that
stopped abruptly as the grenade detonated. Tynan
dived through, tried to spot his target, but saw nothing. He moved to the right, away from the door. He
saw a single person lying near a large chair. Tynan,
keeping his eyes on the figure, moved toward it.
There was a sound from the right, near a chest of
some kind. Tynan spun, firing from the hip. In the
strobelike flashes from the muzzle, he saw a figure
standing there and watched it tossed back by the impact of the bullets. He glanced at the prone figure
and saw it reaching out. Tynan fired once, heard the
round strike soft flesh and snap a bone as the figure
flipped to his back. The wounded man made a stran-
gling sound deep in his throat and kicked one of his
feet, drumming it on the hardwood floor.

For a moment he remained still, waiting for one
of the two downed figures to move. Finally he
stepped to the wall and eased his way closer to the
door. He left the room, keeping his back against the
wall.

From down the hall, he heard a creak and dropped
to the floor as someone there began shooting, the

bullets smashing into the wall where Tynan had been standing. Tynan shot back, aiming at the center of the muzzle flashes. There was a short scream and a thud as someone fell heavily to the floor.

Tynan realized that it was stupid to be up there alone. He had the terrorists trapped on the second floor, he believed. He could back up, return to the first floor, and keep the stairs covered until Arturo and his boys cleared the first floor. That seemed to be the plan of the hour.

Boone and Sterne had no trouble securing the radio room. When Sterne kicked open the door, Boone dived through, rolled once, and came up facing a single man on a cot. Boone whipped his rifle around so that the barrel was pointed at the man's stomach. The terrorist had been trying to draw a pistol from a holster hung on the wall, but froze when he saw that he was covered. Slowly he raised his hands.

Sterne came in then, checked the rest of the small building, but found no one else. There was one wall that was nearly covered with radio equipment, some of it in racks, some of it stacked on a desk, and some of it standing on the floor. Ruby and emerald lights glowed on the panels. There were red numbers burning brightly on a couple of them. A single white light was shining down on the top of a desk that was the main control panel. A file folder that looked like the logbook was open there, a yellow pencil sitting on it. The rest of the room was bare except for a coat tree stuck in the corner.

"Get up," said Boone. "Move away from the pistol." He searched his mind trying to remember some of the Spanish from his high school days, but the only phrase that came to mind was "Manos arriba," but the man had already raised his hands.

With the prisoner standing in the center of the room, Sterne moved to the cot, being careful that he didn't get between Boone and the man. He searched the cot, an old U.S. Army model made of canvas, that was extremely uncomfortable. He took the pistol from the holster and tucked it into his belt.

Boone glanced at the radios. He was trying to figure out the best and fastest way to disable them. It looked like there was a lot of equipment, but much of it was hooked into a single power source, and by destroying that, the equipment would become worthless.

He looked up just as the prisoner jumped at him. Boone swung the barrel of the weapon, trying to hit the man, but missed. They collided and Boone pushed himself free. He dived backward, rolling over against the wall.

Sterne saw the whole thing, and the moment that Boone was clear, fired a short burst. The bullets stitched the man across the chest, small neat holes in front, great fist-sized holes blown out his back, splattering blood on the wall behind him.

Boone got to his feet and walked over to the body. He looked at the spreading pool of blood and then grabbed the man's shirt collar, jerking his back off the floor. "Nice going, asshole," he said to the dead man. "Nice fucking going." He let the man fall back into his own blood.

"Now what?" asked Sterne.

"Let's destroy these radios and then get the fuck out of here." He turned at the sound of firing from the house, but couldn't see anything. He stepped through the door, watching the barn, wondering if there was anyone hiding in there. But there was no sign of activity in the barn.

Arturo and his men moved along the hallway on the main floor. Off to the right, opposite of the staircase, was a set of sliding double doors that were opened. Inside was a library, a large desk, a couple of chairs, and a single floor lamp. They saw no one inside, so they passed it by. They found a door that led to the basement. If Juana Gutierrez was being held in the house, she would probably be imprisoned in the basement. He directed two of his men to cover him while he slowly opened the door. When he learned that it was unlocked, he didn't expect to find anything in the basement, but still he had to check it.

Arturo took two of his flash grenades and flipped one to the man standing on the other side of the door. Both pulled the pins and tossed the grenades down the stairs. They heard them hit the wall and bounce to the floor just before they exploded in a flash of fire and deafening noise.

As that happened, Arturo leaped down the first few steps to the wooden landing. He dropped to his knees, but in the dark windowless basement, he could see nothing around him.

The lights blazed on then as one of the men found a light switch. Arturo jumped from the landing to the dirt of the floor but saw nothing moving down there. He got to his feet and turned to run back up the stairs.

They all moved to the last door at the end of the hallway. Arturo reached out and turned the knob easily. He nodded at his men to alert them. Then, quickly, he shoved open the door and dived through, followed by one of the others. They found themselves in an empty kitchen. Arturo rushed to the table set in a window-enclosed nook. There was a single cup sitting on it, and the coffee was still hot.

He snapped his fingers to get the attention of the men and pointed at the pantry door and then the back door. The men moved to check them out. From upstairs they heard a burst of rifle fire and one of the men dived to the floor as if to avoid being shot before realizing that no one was shooting at him. He got to his feet, grinning sheepishly.

Arturo moved to the windows as there was some answering fire. He heard something or someone fall to the floor, but ignored that for the moment, having his own job to complete. He discovered one of the windows was open, and it appeared that someone had escaped out the back. He hoped that Tynan's man there had stopped the fleeing terrorist. He then heard a burst from out back where Jones hid. Arturo leaped to the window but was too late to see anything out there, including the muzzle flashes and bouncing tracers.

The shooting upstairs stopped for the moment. Arturo moved to the door and yelled for his men to follow him. They ran back into the hallway and found Tynan crouched on the steps, watching the second floor.

"I've got them trapped up there," Tynan said. "I got one of them and there are a couple more barricaded. I've no idea how many there are."

"What do you think we should do?" asked Arturo.

Tynan looked at his watch. He could tell from the increasing light in the house that the sun was up. He had noticed that the ground around the house was clear, meaning that the occupants had good fields of fire in all directions. It also meant, with the sun out, that no one in the house could escape into the night.

"We've got to do something to clear the building," said Tynan.

"I think that we fall back to a secondary position and burn the place. It's the quickest and safest way," said Arturo.

"Yes," agreed Tynan, "but it doesn't allow us to search for the clues we need to find the generalissimo's daughter since she hasn't turned up here yet. The first thing we have to do is clear the house. We just can't leave those people running around loose up there."

"So what do we do?"

Tynan moved back, off the steps. "We assault the corridor. Roll a flash grenade into it and storm the place as it goes off. I saw six doors up there. Three on each side of the hall. We hit each one of them within seconds of the grenade going off in the hall. The first room on the right has already been cleared. When we finish that, we re-form and take the next level."

Arturo nodded and said, "Good." Rapidly he translated the instructions into Spanish. Each of the three men with him took one of the flash grenades and pulled the pins.

"We are ready," said Arturo.

Tynan began to slowly move up the steps again. He held the pistol grip of his M-16 in his right hand and the flash grenade in his left hand. When he reached the landing and could see into the hallway again, he threw the grenade and dropped until he heard it detonate, and the concussion from it washed over him. He leaped up the remaining steps, kicked the first door to the left from its hinges, and threw in a second grenade. He flattened against the wall as Arturo rushed past him to smash the next door.

As the grenade exploded in a crash of breaking glass and smoke boiled out the door, Tynan dived in on his stomach. The lone occupant was standing behind an overturned chest, his hands clapped to his ears. Blood ran from his nose and mouth and down his neck, staining his bare chest crimson. He seemed no longer to understand where he was or what was happening. His weapon lay at his feet.

Tynan moved toward him carefully, and when he didn't respond Tynan kicked his feet out from under him and then tried to punt his head through the window. The man lost consciousness with a grunt of pain.

It was then that Tynan heard the shooting going on. He heard a startled scream and the crash of a body hitting the floor. He got to his belly and crawled forward, peeking around the corner. Two of Arturo's men were firing up the stairs that led to the next floor, the third man lay on the carpeting holding his stomach.

Tynan got to his feet and stepped into the hallway. The room opposite him was burning, the flames licking at the bedspread and the legs of a dresser. A body was sprawled on the floor, blood pooling around it.

"We can't get up the stairs," Arturo reported to him.

"Doesn't matter," said Tynan. "If they had the girl, they would be trying to bargain their way clear with her. Have your guys withdraw. Put a guard up here for a moment while we check out the library. See what papers we can find." He pointed into the burning room. "We'll let the fire take care of them."

Arturo called softly to his men. They both fired a burst up the stairs and then leaped back, dragging the body of the wounded man with them. He screamed as they jerked at his arms and he left a trail of blood on the hardwood floor. As they reached the steps, the screaming stopped abruptly and the man went limp, dying suddenly.

Arturo detailed one man to stay as the rest of them raced down the stairs. Tynan and Arturo went into the library. Tynan felt along the wall until he found the light switch and turned it on. It was a momentary shock to see the bright overhead lights, but there was no reason not to use them now. Tynan went to the desk and sat in the high-backed chair behind it. He pulled on the center drawer and found that it was locked. He took his knife, put the point against the metal of the lock, and shoved. There was a splintering of wood, but the drawer would not open. Finally he took his pistol and put a single round into the center of the lock and jerked the drawer free. He dumped the contents on the top of the desk, reading through the papers quickly.

Arturo had forced a closet door and found a filing cabinet hidden inside. He dragged it out into the room and opened the top drawer. He found hundreds of file folders. "It's going to take a week to work through all this stuff," he said.

"Granted, if we have to look at it all. We have to ignore everything that doesn't relate to our problem." He tried to open another drawer and found that it too was locked. "Shit." He used his knife again and forced the drawer. Inside he found a handgun, ammunition for it, and a cleaning kit. Slowly he worked his way down one side of the desk, breaking into it as he went. He dumped the contents into the pile of papers he had created on the desktop. He was suddenly aware of the room beginning to fill with smoke.

From the hallway came a burst of fire. First it seemed that one of the terrorists had opened fire and then Pablo shot back. There was a moment of quiet and then a long final burst.

Arturo leaped around the file cabinet and hit the wall by the door. "Pablo," he hissed. "You okay?"

"Yes. I'm fine," he called down from the landing. "I saw one of them, but he decided that he did not really want to come down here."

"Keep your eyes opened." Arturo turned his attention back to Tynan. "We have got to get out of here."

Tynan nodded. It was getting late and there was more smoke in the room. It was becoming hard to see and hard to breathe. Tynan was afraid that there might be some kind of routine report that signaled everything was fine in the camp, and if it didn't come, more terrorists might arrive. Or the men who held the generalissimo's daughter might decide that she had outlived her usefulness. He fumbled through the papers, searching for anything that would give him a clue. He tossed them aside when they proved useless. He was afraid that he would never find what he needed. That he would have to go somewhere else to search for clues. And then he turned over the map.

At first it meant nothing. Just a map of the surrounding countryside. Then he noticed light markings on it in blue and red. He studied them carefully, realized that they were approach and escape routes for a mountain location, one that was nearby.

"That's it," he said. "I've got it. Let's get out." He jumped to his feet, but wasn't certain that he had it. All he could do was hope that it was the clue he needed because there wasn't time to search for a new one. He could barely see because of the smoke curling through the room. He could hear the crackle of flames and he could hear Arturo coughing badly. He ran to the door and watched Pablo retreating down the stairs, the flames leaping after him.

11

Tynan ran to the porch and stopped just outside the door, standing protected under the overhang. He could see heavy dense smoke swirling around the ground as more of the house caught fire. He watched as two of Arturo's men leaped to the ground and sprinted toward the shot-up hulk of the car, diving behind it, out of sight. No one shot at them.

Tynan made a long count and then dropped to the ground, running toward the radio shack. There was a single shot behind him that kicked up dirt to his left. He ignored it as Boone and Sterne, crouching in the doorway of his destination, opened fire on full automatic, pumping rounds into the third-floor windows. Strangely, Tynan's attention was focused on the brass being ejected from their M-16s in a cascade of copper flashes. He ran past them and dived into the radio shack, nearly landing on the body of the dead terrorist.

Both Boone and Sterne stopped the covering fire as Tynan ran by them. Boone withdrew to the dark confines of the radio room, Sterne staying close to the door, watching the upper floor windows.

"Now what, Skipper?" said Sterne over his shoulder. He could see someone moving in the upper story of the house, running past the windows.

He couldn't tell how many people were up there or what they were doing.

"We have to take the barn and search that damned blockhouse out back and we have to do it quickly."

"What about the guys still in the house?" asked Sterne.

"I don't think they're going to be much of a threat to us," said Tynan.

There was a muffled explosion followed by a series of minor detonations and a long, loud sighing. For a moment there was silence and then another explosion.

"Jesus!" said Sterne.

Tynan stepped to the door in time to see the roof of the house, smoke pouring from a dozen holes in it, and flames shooting from several others, fold up and collapse as a fountain of sparks shot into the sky. There were screams from the house, one of them cut off suddenly, and then the walls seemed to disintegrate, falling outward, scattering burning debris all over the ground.

"Okay," said Tynan, turning away from the doorway. "That takes care of the terrorists in the house. Now I want you and Boone to get around to the back of the barn. Arturo and I will toss a couple of flash grenades in the front and when they detonate, we'll go in."

"That's a pretty big area," said Sterne. "Grenades won't do much good."

"Probably not," agreed Tynan, "but when they explode, it'll draw everyone's attention to them for a split second. Give us a little cover when we go in."

"Aye aye, Skipper," said Sterne. "Give us a couple of minutes to get into position."

Tynan nodded and Sterne peeked out the door. He saw no one moving anywhere near the remains of the house, the barn, or the three cars. He pushed himself out the door and ran across the open ground, dodging around the flaming debris scattered by the house. He ran to the far side of the barn, used it for cover, and disappeared from sight.

Boone took off next. He hit the side of the barn and stopped long enough to glance in one of the big windows. He ducked back, signaled that he had seen nothing of interest inside, and then vanished around a corner just as Sterne had.

Tynan stepped into the open, pointed at Arturo, and waved him forward. Tynan then ran for the front of the barn, glancing up to see smoke beginning to appear on the barn's roof, another fire started when the house collapsed.

In seconds Tynan was leaning against the front of the barn, his breath coming in gasps because of the run across the open area. He just couldn't get used to the altitude. He worked his way to the right, along the rough unpainted wood, toward a small dirty window, and tried to look inside, but the rising sun made it nearly impossible to see anything without exposing himself to any terrorists who might be hiding. He crouched, moved under the window, and looked in the other side, but still could see nothing in there.

Near the window was a small door that had a wooden latch. It appeared that the door opened outward, and that meant it was probably not locked. Arturo hit the barn then and Tynan pointed at the latch. Arturo nodded his understanding.

Tynan pulled the last of his flash grenades out and glanced at Arturo, who reached over and grabbed the latch, lifting slowly, carefully. Tynan pulled the pins, then, holding a grenade in each hand, nodded. He spun and tossed one grenade through the window. He hesitated and sent the second after the first. A moment later there was an explosion that blew out the rest of the windows in the barn. The second detonated, shaking the whole structure, causing dirt to cascade from the rafters.

As the grenades went off, Arturo jerked out the door and ran through. Tynan followed, saw a large post in front of him, and dived around it, landing in a pile of hay that stunk of manure. He rolled behind the edge of a stall and surveyed his surroundings. Smoke was beginning to billow from a stall several feet away where one of the grenades had detonated, igniting the straw in the flash of fire.

There was a shout from the other end of the barn as both Sterne and Boone entered. Tynan rose up and saw one of them diving from cover. From above them came a single shot that slammed into the side of the barn, but not coming close to any of the men.

To his left, Tynan saw Arturo crawling along the side of a Lincoln Continental that had a cracked windshield and a flat rear tire. Arturo pointed up, toward the loft and at the ladder that led up to it.

Tynan waved him forward and then got to his knees. He aimed his M-16 upward, at the floor of the loft, and fired the rest of the magazine into it. The wood splintered and dust mushroomed from it.

Arturo leaped to his feet and sprinted to the ladder, rolling to cover in a stall that was opposite it. He crouched there, his back against the flimsy wood. He looked up, stretching his neck, searching for the gunman who had fired, but could see nothing of

him. He sprayed the area around the ladder with a
long burst, saw bits of wood splintering and flying
about and sawdust swirling, but could not spot the
terrorist.

Before he could move, Sterne appeared and dived
behind the ladder. He checked the loft opposite him,
and then swung around so he could scramble up the
ladder. As he moved upward, Boone jumped forward, firing into the loft to cover Sterne as Sterne
disappeared from sight.

Above him Tynan heard Sterne moving around.
Suddenly Sterne shouted, "Jesus Christ!" and someone fired a five-shot burst. Tynan was on his feet,
running across the floor of the barn. He jumped to the
ladder and scrambled up it. He leaped into the loft,
spun, and saw Sterne standing over a body.

"I got her," he said, his voice soft and shaky.
He knelt down and pulled the fatigue hat from her
head, revealing long black hair. "I got her," he repeated.

Tynan moved closer and looked at the body.
She was wearing surplus U.S. Army fatigues. The
sleeves had been hacked from the jacket to reveal
slender, golden arms. He could see a line of bullet
holes, a little blood staining them, across her chest.
Sterne had hit her with four of his five shots. Not
bad shooting from the hip.

Sterne reached out to touch her long hair. He
brushed it lightly from her forehead and then turned
to Tynan. "I didn't know it was a girl."

Tynan knelt and picked up a long-barreled Colt
revolver from where it had fallen in the hay. "She
had this and managed to fire it at us."

"Yes, sir," said Sterne, getting to his feet. He
stood motionless for a moment, and then kicked the

dead girl in the side, the blow lifting her slightly. He turned then and headed for the ladder.

As Sterne started climbing down, Tynan began searching the dead girl's pockets. He gingerly picked at the pocket flaps of her fatigue shirt, trying to avoid feeling her. He turned his head away so that he couldn't see what he was doing, and then felt ridiculous. The woman was dead and would never know what happened to her body. Tynan clenched his teeth as if trying to prevent himself from being sick and quickly checked all her pockets. He found nothing in them except a single piece of paper with a message written in Spanish. He could pick out enough words to realize that it was some kind of lover's note and had no tactical value. He put it back.

He climbed down the ladder, dropping the last four feet to the floor. He noticed that the smoke was beginning to fill the barn as it had the house. He ran to the door, turned a final time, and stared at the Lincoln Continental. It looked almost new and Tynan wondered where the terrorists had gotten it.

Outside he learned that Arturo's men had broken into the small square building and it turned out to be an arms locker. They had dragged some of the material out. They had found AK-47s, boxes of Chicom grenades—including some rocket-propelled grenades—pistols, ammunition, and a single SAM-7 shoulder-fired antiaircraft missile.

"Put that stuff back inside," said Tynan.

"What? Are you leaving it for the terrorists? You're not going to do that, are you?" asked Boone.

"Of course not. Put it back inside and we'll blow it up," said Tynan.

"What about souvenirs?" asked Sterne.

"You guys won't be able to get anything back to the States except a couple of the pistols. Customs will take the automatic weapons and grenades," said Tynan.

Sterne moved to the door and said, "A pistol is fine with me."

"Have your boys take whatever they want," he said to Arturo. "Consider it a partial payment for the assistance." He thought for a moment and said, "And drag a box of those grenades out here."

As the men disappeared into the arms room to collect their souvenirs, Tynan looked at the sun and then his watch. They had been screwing around for nearly two hours. One thing just led to another and he didn't see any end to it. They would have to do something more to the radio room. A couple of grenades in the door to destroy the radios. And the cars. He couldn't just leave them sitting there. Odds were that the locals would move in and pick them clean, but there was the possibility that the terrorists would come back to claim all that was salvageable. He wanted to leave them nothing of value. But it all took time, and they still didn't know where the girl was being held or if she was still alive.

He tapped Arturo on the shoulder and said, "Have a couple of your men burn the cars. Four or five rounds into the fuel tanks, and toss a grenade into the gas."

Arturo issued the orders in Spanish and four men ran toward the cars. They stopped fifteen or twenty feet away and opened fire, spraying the cars with rifle fire, shattering the glass in the windows and headlights, punching through the metal of the doors to rip up the interior, rocking the cars and stripping bits of chrome and steel from them.

One of the men moved to the front of the closest car and fired into the radiator which exploded into a fountain of rusty water. The hood sprang up and was ripped away. He stopped shooting, walked to the side, and put five rounds into the side that flattened the tires and penetrated the fuel tank so that the gas bubbled out into the dirt. A moment later flames created by one of the tracer rounds raced along the spilled fuel and set the rear of the vehicle ablaze.

As all three of the cars began to burn, Boone touched Tynan on the shoulder and said, "Say, Skipper, I found a box of plastique in there along with the detonators. I could rig something up to blow up the arms locker easily. Wouldn't take all that long."

"They kept the detonators and explosives in the same room?" said Tynan.

"Yeah, well, sometimes the training isn't as good as it could be," said Boone. "Anyway, they've left everything I need in there."

"Then go to it." He looked at Arturo. "Get your men together and get ready to get out of here." He pulled the map from his breast pocket and crouched down to examine it. There were five places marked on it. He checked it against his own map, figuring the distances and directions to the closest of the terrorist camps. It seemed that the best way to operate was to take them one at a time, starting with the closest of them.

Arturo returned and Tynan showed him the map. "I make it about five or six klicks to the next camp," he said, pointing.

"We could be there in an hour, hour and a half, if we push hard," said Arturo. "Terrain isn't that bad. Just a couple of hills to climb."

"Let's get moving," said Tynan. "Arturo, take the point." He turned as Boone left the arms locker. "If you're ready, you can take up the rear and I'll take the slack."

"All set," said Boone. "Left a time-delay fuse. Should go up in about twenty minutes. We'll be able to hear it so we'll know if it blows."

They moved out then, walking up the slope to the south, following a narrow path that wound toward the top. They climbed it quickly, reached the crest, and descended into the next valley. Arturo kept the pace steady and within minutes Tynan found himself breathing hard and sweating heavily. He used the butt of his rifle as a walking stick.

As they reached the valley floor, they heard a rumble in the distance that signaled that the arms locker had blown up. There was a gigantic explosion followed by several smaller detonations. The patrol stopped and looked back, but could see nothing because of the hills.

Shortly after that, as they crossed the valley, Arturo stopped, sitting on the bank of a small, crystal-clear stream. He reached out with a cupped hand and took a drink of the ice-cold water. He waited there while the rest of the patrol caught up to him.

Tynan flopped down on his back, staring into the deep blue of the sky, trying to catch his breath. He turned his head and looked at the sun climbing higher. He knew that they had to hurry but he wasn't sure how much longer he could go on. Sweat was pouring from him because of the effort of walking in the high mountains.

"We should go," said Arturo.

Tynan groaned and sat up. He looked at the next ridge. It seemed to climb into the sky. It seemed to be insurmountable. It seemed that it would be impossible to reach the top of it. It was just too high.

Tynan forced himself to his feet, leaned on his rifle, and said, "Lead on."

Again they moved out, working their way up the hill. At the top, Arturo stopped long enough for Tynan to catch him. He pointed down and said, "That is the first place marked on your map."

Tynan's reaction was to drop to his belly, but then he realized that Arturo was still standing. The place was obviously deserted. There was a single dilapidated house below them. Part of the roof had fallen in and the back door hung from a bottom hinge. Huge weeds had grown up around the door and the path leading to it. The windows seemed to have been broken out, the bits of glass twinkling in the sun. Although they kept a close watch on it for nearly ten minutes, Tynan using his binoculars, they saw no movement anywhere near it.

"One down and four to go," said Tynan as he took out the map.

"Maybe we should allow the men to eat something before we move out again," said Arturo.

"Right," said Tynan, nodding. "Tell them to eat quickly if they've brought something with them. We can't waste a lot of time around here."

"What about the cars?" asked Arturo. "Shouldn't we send someone back for them?"

Tynan sat up and looked at the group of men. He had no idea how many terrorists would be in the camp if they found the girl. He did know that good military doctrine dictated that he not split his forces until he knew the size and distribution of the enemy. If they found it necessary to attack the terrorists, he would probably need every man he had.

"It's a good thought," he said, "but I want to keep us together until we have an idea about the enemy."

"I understand," said Arturo.

As he ran off to pass out his instructions, Tynan sat down to read his map. He could see that the next camp was about ten klicks away, but the one after that was nearly seventy. There was no way he could get to it on foot, and he wondered if he had been right in keeping his group together. They would need the cars to get to it and it would take a half a day to get back to them. Then he remembered that Custer had tried to cover all the bets at Little Big Horn. It simply meant that the next camp would have to be the right one.

Tynan got to his feet and moved down the hill. By midafternoon they could be in position. If it was the wrong place, they would have to call things off until the next day. It would take them a long time to get ready for another raid. But if it was the right one, they could have the problem resolved by nightfall.

Without a word, Arturo waved the men to their feet and then fell in on the path. They began their climb again, reached the ridge, and followed the path around the top of it, past a grove of trees and then down into another valley. They could see the path leading back up another mountain in the distance, and Tynan wondered if they would ever find the end of it. The trail seemed to go on forever.

12

The path finally disintegrated near the top of a ridge, fanning out into the trees and bushes and grassy meadows. Tynan and Arturo climbed to the top of the ridge and looked down into yet another valley. Far below them they could see a lone cabin with a pathway that led away from the door, sheltered by trees on both sides. Tynan was going to suggest that there was nothing of interest below them when he caught a flash of movement in the trees far south of the cabin. He pulled his binoculars from their case and studied the trees where he had seen the movement. In the shadows of the trees he finally spotted a single man dressed in dark clothing that resembled a military uniform, although Tynan thought that the resemblance might be wishful thinking on his part.

He tapped Arturo on the shoulder, handed him the binoculars, and then pointed. A moment later Arturo nodded and said, "I see him." He moved the binoculars so that they were on the cabin. "What do you think?" he asked.

Tynan took the binoculars back and studied the cabin. After nearly a minute, he thought he saw movement behind one of the windows. Then a man left the cabin, walked down the path, and disappeared into the trees. He emerged within seconds with another man, and together they returned to the cabin. A third man waited for them at the door.

"I don't believe that it is a poor farmer's house," said Tynan.

"No, my friend, you are wrong. The house belongs to a farmer, I just don't see him or his family. By this time, he would be tending his fields. There is no one working outside and there are too many men."

"I suppose we better check it out," said Tynan. He got the map he had found out of his pocket. He oriented it carefully and studied the scene laid out below him. It seemed that the landmarks agreed with the map. "This has got to be the right place," he said.

"Yes," agreed Arturo, "but there is something wrong down there."

Tynan looked at the hillside sloping away from them. A light forest covered most of it. Near the cabin the forest ended and the area was spotted with small clumps of trees and bushes. Far to the right there was a long, fat finger of forest that touched the valley floor and disappeared in the distance. To the left the slope was a green meadow sprinkled with flowers and some boulders. A clear brook bubbled through the meadow to a shallow pool fifty feet from the cabin.

As they watched, another man appeared in the distance, walking slowly along the path toward the cabin. He stopped once and turned his head as if to speak to someone hidden in the trees. Then he continued his journey, and when he was near the front door, another man came out and greeted him.

"Christ," said Tynan, "there's got to be nine thousand people down there."

"What do we do?" asked Arturo.

"There is too much open ground for us to cover in the daylight." He checked his watch. "Should be dark in a couple of hours. Gives us a chance to move into position and hit the place about dusk. We have to get right in because if they know what's coming, they're going to kill the girl. We have to be through the front door before they know we're around."

Arturo nodded.

Tynan looked back over his shoulder and then at the cabin again. "I would think we've got to use every opening. Hit the door and windows at the same time. All of them." He used the binoculars again to survey the cabin and said, "How many rooms in that cabin?"

Arturo shrugged. "It might be just one big room or it might be divided into two, three, or four. Rooms have become the big status symbol in Ecuador. The more rooms you have, the richer you are."

"That's great. We'll just have to hit all the windows too, then." He pushed himself backward, away from the ridge line, and then crawled to where the men waited. He explained to them what they planned to do and how they wanted to assault the cabin. He showed them the map and used it to illustrate the approaches. He wrapped up his speech by saying, "We'll have about an hour to study the cabin before we make the attack. Any questions?"

No one asked any. They knew all the answers from the raid on the terrorist camp. The people in the cabin, with one exception, were considered to be the enemy, and if they resisted, they would be killed. They would not shoot to wound, or aim for legs or shoulders. No one asked about prisoners, and Tynan suddenly wondered what he would do with any if they managed to take some. He hadn't even considered the question when they hit the terrorist camp. Turning them over to the Ecuadoran government for prosecution would make the most sense. Except governments had a bad habit of releasing terrorists, which only encouraged them to return to their terrorist activities.

"Arturo," said Tynan, "why don't you take the point and lead the way. Boone, take the slack and I'll bring up the rear. Remember, we can't make any noise that might give us away. We have to get into position without the terrorists knowing we're out here."

Arturo nodded and moved to the south until he disappeared into the trees with Boone following him. The men strung out behind them, five or ten meters between them, each now carrying his weapon in his hands at the ready. He noticed that the locals glided through the trees with a second sense. They made no noise and seemed to avoid the dried leaves and broken twigs with a psychic ability.

Tynan slid up behind Sterne and whispered to him, "You don't have to worry about snakes. I think we're too high for them. They can't survive at these altitudes."

"Sure, Skipper," said Sterne.

Tynan dropped back, watched the last of the men enter the trees, and then followed. These woods were not thick like the jungles of Southeast Asia or even South America. They were thin, with a thick layer of needles from the evergreens carpeting the ground, cushioning their feet and reducing any noise they might have made. There were lots of thin trees, the leaves rustling in the light, cool breeze that dried the sweat caused by the sun. Tynan found himself suddenly shivering with the cold, but ignored the feeling.

The pace up the hill was rapid. Arturo made as much time as he could until he reached the ridge line. Before crossing it, he halted to study the forest in front of him. He moved deeper into it so that there would be no possibility of someone accidentally seeing them. Happy with that, he began the descent, the pace now slow as each of the men watched the path for twigs that could snap or bushes that could rustle loud enough to give them away.

In an hour, Arturo estimated that they were due east of the cabin, maybe half a klick or a little more from it. He waved the men to cover and began moving to the west until the trees thinned enough for him to see into the meadows surrounding their objective.

A moment later, as Arturo crouched at the edge of the forest, Tynan crept up beside him and leaned so close that his lips nearly touched Arturo's ear. "What do you think?"

Arturo shrugged and continued to study the cabin. For a moment there was no sound around them except the birds overhead and the animals running through the forest. Then there was a shout from the cabin—a woman's voice that changed into a scream of anguish.

Juana Gutierrez had been dragged from the closet and shoved into a chair. Her whole body ached from having been tied in one position for so long. There was pain in her chest where she had been beaten, along her thighs where she had been clawed, and in her abdomen from having been raped. When the hands had reached into the darkness and grabbed her, she hadn't resisted because she knew that she could do nothing about it.

She was forced into a chair, her bound hands lifted over the back of it as a rope was tied to her wrists and fastened to the rung there between the legs of the chair. Her legs were untied and then re-tied, her ankles roped to the chair so that her feet were apart and her knees spread. There was no way for her to conceal her nakedness.

The man who tied her into the chair reached out to pull and pinch at her breasts and nipples, laughing. "You like this, don't you?" he asked in a harsh whisper. When she didn't respond, he rubbed her belly and then tugged at her pubic hair until she cried out once, sharply.

"Get away from her," barked one of the other men. He set a field phone on the table and said, "Your father has not cooperated with our requests, so we are going to make a recording to send to him. The pictures of your plight have made no apparent impression on him. He is a very hard man, but maybe the sound of your pain will convince him that we are serious."

He took the wires from the field phone and taped one of them to her breast, making sure that the bare copper wire touched her nipple. Then, slowly, he taped the other to the inside of her thigh, the ex-posed wire reaching up to touch her in her most sensitive areas. Finished, he stood over her and smiled showing his broken yellow teeth. He turned and nodded to one of the other men who pushed the record button on the battery-powered tape recorder.

"Now we begin," said the man. "Is there some-thing you would like to say to your father? No? Well, let's see if we can't get you to say some-thing."

He moved to the field phone, took hold of the crank, and waited until the girl's eyes were on his. He gave the handle a half crank and was pleased with her yelp.

"Very good," he said. "Very good indeed. Now let's see if we can make the song last a little longer, my dear. Are you ready?"

He spun the crank then, letting the current surge through her body. She began to scream as her muscles tightened because of the electricity. She threw her head back so that they could see the pulsing of her heartbeat in the veins at her throat. She strained at the ropes, unconsciously pulling at them so that they bit deeply into her wrists, ankles, and knees, breaking the skin. Blood dribbled down her hands to spot the floor behind her. It ran down her calves and from her ankles.

The current stopped suddenly and she dropped back into the chair, but it came again, making her try to leap up. She was effectively restrained and could not escape. The muscles of her thighs, stomach, and chest rippled under her skin so that it seemed that they were etched in stone. Sweat beaded her forehead and ran down her sides. She screamed again and again until the current stopped.

She collapsed into the chair, her head hanging down, her chin nearly on her chest as she breathed rapidly, trying to catch her breath.

Another naked woman appeared in the doorway that led to the bedroom, drawn to the front room by the screams of the prisoner. She leaned against the wall, watching the torture of the captive woman. She was not concerned that the men in the cabin could see her naked because most of them had their eyes locked on the captive anyway. She ran her fingers through her long, dark hair and licked her lips as the man turned the crank of the field phone. She liked the way the girl went rigid, her muscles etched against her skin. She felt a flutter of excitement in her belly as she watched the captive respond to the electricity and the sweat of pain and fear run down her face and her sides to drip to the floor to mingle with the blood.

"Would you like to speak to your father?" the man asked Juana kindly.

She began to babble then, pleading with them to stop, pleading with her father to do anything they wanted, pleading with God to strike her dead so that pain would stop.

The man grinned and let her ramble on, pleading with everyone. When he tired of it, he spun the crank and watched her try to leap out of the chair, the strain nearly snapping her bones. He fell back into his chair, laughing hard. Finally he said, "Shut off the tape machine."

The girl thought that the ordeal was over for the moment, but the man wasn't through with her. He stepped close to her and punched her once in the stomach, and before she could catch her breath, spun the crank. He kept at it, giving her no chance to rest, no chance to breathe. She could no longer scream, and it was only minutes before she passed out.

Outside, hidden in the trees, Arturo listened to the girl's screams with growing agitation. He wanted to move in immediately, freeing the girl from her tormentors, but Tynan held him back, telling him that they would be hard-pressed to cover the open ground before someone saw them. To try would be to sign the girl's death warrant. To try would be to force the terrorists to react. So they sat listening.

For half an hour, Tynan stared at the cabin, as if he could see inside it. Each time the screaming stopped, he hoped that he had heard the last of it, and each time it started again, it burned into him. He too wanted to rush the cabin, but he didn't want to see the girl die. Listening to her screams was hard enough.

When the sun had dipped below the horizon and as the light faded rapidly, the door of the cabin opened and a lone man left. He hurried along the path without glancing back or looking to the right or left. He disappeared from sight as the screaming began inside. Moments later it died and was not resumed.

Now that it was finally dark, Tynan moved deeper into the trees, toward where his men crouched. To Sterne he said, "I want you to take one man and cover the back. When you hear us toss a flash grenade in the front, you do the same in the back. Then neutralize everyone you see."

"By neutralize do you mean . . ."

"By neutralize I mean to take them out of the action. If you must kill them to do it, then kill them. Do not do anything to endanger yourself or the man with you. Better a bunch of dead terrorists than one of us dead."

"Aye aye, Skipper."

At that moment Arturo appeared. He said, "I think that it is time that we hit the cabin."

Tynan nodded and said, "Boone, I want you with me on the front. You take one of the windows. Arturo, you take the other and I'll go through the door." He pointed to a couple of Arturo's men. "You and you cover the windows on this side. You two others take the windows on the far side. The rest of you fan out across the path and kill anyone who tries to approach from that direction. You're going to operate as a rear guard. Any questions?''

When none was asked, Tynan said, ''We go in three minutes. Keep low and to the shadows. Hold when you are in place until you hear us initiate the action.''

That done, they dropped their extra equipment, their canteens, their souvenirs captured in the terrorists' camp, their binoculars and machetes, and moved to the edge of the woods. They spread out there and Tynan hesitated, studying the ground directly in front of him. It sloped downward to a low point and then there was a slight rise with the cabin on it. Lights burned in all the windows, but little of it escaped to push back the night. There was enough debris, fallen trees, boulders, logs, and waste that there was plenty of cover now that the sun was gone. Tynan got to his belly and inched his way from the trees, his weapons cradled in his arms, watching the cabin, the ground in front of him and the men around him.

He reached a fallen log and lay against it, peeking around the end. He saw a shadow pass the window, but the man didn't stop to look out. A moment later it happened again, but apparently the men in the cabin felt safe, believing that the guards at the far end of the valley would protect them. Tynan moved around the log, crawling forward through the tender grass until he descended into the depression around the house. The bottom of it was damp and he could feel the water seeping through his clothes, soaking his skin. The water was cold.

Once through the bottom of the depression and on the upward slope, Tynan stopped for a moment. He surveyed the cabin. Through the window he could see little except the beams that held up the roof and a bare electric light bulb swinging on its wires. He wondered where they got the power because he didn't hear a generator. He decided that it wasn't important enough to worry about and began to crawl forward until he reached the base of the wall. Then, feeling safe for the first time, he relaxed slightly, taking time to wipe his face and brush at the mud smeared on the front of his shirt.

He saw Arturo reach the wall, so Tynan began to crawl along it until he came to the corner. He peeked around and saw that the cabin door was open. He looked along the path and saw one of the men standing in the cool night air smoking a cigarette, the orange tip describing small ovals as he shook his hand for some reason.

From inside he could hear voices, some of them speaking rapid-fire Spanish that was too fast for Tynan to understand. Some of them deeper in the cabin were speaking English, and although he could tell that one of the voices was feminine, he couldn't hear the words.

The smoking man tossed his cigarette away and spun, moving rapidly to the cabin. There was a flash of light as the door opened and closed. As soon as the man was inside, Tynan worked his way around the corner. Both Arturo and Boone followed him closely.

Tynan stopped near the door and waved Boone past him to take his place under the window there. Arturo was set and, still crouched, had gotten to his feet. Tynan did the same, thought about trying the knob, and then realized that anyone inside would be sure to see it turn. He got to his feet, leaning against the wall of the cabin. He could see nothing through the window without moving his head far enough to become visible to anyone inside.

He glanced right and left and saw that both men were ready. Twenty feet in front of him, he saw the rest of the men spreading out to cover the path to prevent a counterattack. He nodded to let both men know he was about to move. He spun then, kicked out, hitting the door near the knob, splintering it. He tossed in a single flash grenade and flattened himself on the ground. As it exploded, he was on his feet, diving through the door and the boiling smoke, rolling to his shoulder and coming up in a kneeling position.

In front of him he saw a single terrorist, dressed in a flowered shirt and khaki pants, groping for a rifle leaning in the corner. The man had one hand scrubbing at his face, smearing the blood that poured from his nose. Tynan fired once and the round caught the man chest high, flipping him back to hit the counter with the makeshift sink. He slipped to the floor, blood spurting in a crimson geyser.

Tynan spun and saw another man taking aim at him, but before he could react or the man could shoot, the window disintegrated as Arturo fired a short burst through it. The man pitched forward, smashing into the chair where Juana Gutierrez had been bound earlier. He rolled to his back, a hand clawing weakly at his wounds. He spasmed once, his legs stiffening, and he died with a growl deep in his throat.

There was one other man in the room, but he had frozen as he had reached for his weapon and heard all the firing around him. Tynan covered him, and the man straightened slowly and raised his hands in surrender.

There was the sound of breaking glass from the rear of the cabin, and Tynan looked up as the door that led into another room opened. A pistol was tossed out and landed on the floor near Tynan's feet. Then a man appeared, his hands clasped tightly together on top of his head. He wore no shirt, shoes, or socks, and it looked as if he had hastily scrambled back into his pants.

A woman appeared behind him, her hands clasped at the base of her neck, hidden under her long dark hair. Her skirt was disheveled, the zipper near her hip unfastened, and her blouse was completely unbuttoned and hung free outside the waistband. She stopped short, staring at Tynan.

"Christ!" he said. "Hamilton!"

She smiled slyly, winked, and said, "Had you fooled too, didn't I?"

"No," he said sadly, shaking his head. "Disappointed me, but didn't fool me."

Boone entered then, moving toward the man who had tried to grab a weapon. He searched him and pushed him out of the way, moving toward the man who wore only his pants, but being careful that he didn't get between Tynan and the terrorists. He patted the man down, rubbing his hands along the man's legs. He did not ignore the crotch. Because too many men had been killed because they had been squeamish about searching there for a weapon. Before he could search Hamilton, more people entered the tiny front room.

Arturo entered and covered the prisoners with his weapon. Tynan moved to the closet and slowly opened the door. A powerful stench, a residue from the prisoner who had been held in it for days without the benefit of sanitary facilities, hit him in the face like the odor of a garbage scow. He saw Gutierrez sitting on the floor, her hands bound behind her, her knees tied together and a rope leading from them and looped around her neck. He pulled his knife from the scabbard and cut the rope, but she didn't move.

Tynan set his weapon down, being careful to keep the receiver off the dirt, now that there were others in the cabin to cover the prisoners. He reached in and gently lifted the girl to her feet. Carefully he cut the rope that encircled her knees and then the one around her ankles. He pulled her forward, out of the closet, and cut the ropes around her elbows and wrists. She stood there, her eyes vacant and staring as if she was unaware of what was happening to her, as if waiting for the horror to begin again.

"Get something to cover her," he said.

Boone came from the bedroom, a large quilt in his hands. "This is all I could find back in there, Skipper."

"It should do just fine for the time being," said Tynan as he draped it around the naked girl. He eased her to one of the chairs, and then had to force her to sit down. He turned to stare at Hamilton. "Why do it?" he asked her, his eyes still on the captive girl.

"Because the government here is totally corrupt," she sneered.

"Fuck!" said Tynan. "That's your excuse for torturing an innocent girl?"

"She's not so innocent. Her father is—"

"I really don't give a fuck who her father is," said Tynan, shaking his head. "That's no justification for what's been done in here."

The girl screamed then as the circulation returned to her feet and hands and the pain coursed through her. Everyone turned to look.

Hamilton moved then. She drew the .25-caliber automatic hidden under her hair and fired once at Boone who stood next to her. The round hit him on the side of the head, stunning him, and he fell to his hands and knees.

Tynan heard the quiet pop of the miniature pistol and dumped the girl to the floor, out of the line of fire. He dived in the other direction, snagging his weapon as he moved. He rolled to his back, and as the barrel found its target he pulled the trigger three times.

The rounds smashed into Hamilton's stomach, lifting her from her feet and driving her back into the flimsy wall of the cabin. She choked out a startled scream and collapsed to the floor, leaving a smear of blood behind her where the bullets had punched through her back. She sprawled on the floor, her head resting on the wall, her hair stained with her own blood.

Tynan glanced at the girl who was now pulling the quilt around herself tightly, sobbing almost hysterically. Boone had sat down, one hand on his head where the bullet had hit him, but obviously not badly hurt.

Tynan got to his feet and moved to Hamilton. Her midsection was drenched in blood and it was beginning to pool under her. Her blouse had pulled open so that he could see two of the bullet holes in her smooth skin, the edges bruised. There was little bleeding around the entrance wounds. The real damage had been done as the rounds punched through her back. Tynan reached out to feel her throat and felt a weak, thready pulse.

As he touched her, she opened her eyes and smiled weakly. She tried to move, failed, and said haltingly, "You had your chance to find out how good I was in bed last night, but you blew it."

"Nope," said Tynan seriously. "I was afraid of what I might catch from you." He saw that her face was getting a waxy look that meant she was dying. Her eyes were unfocused and staring upward.

She opened her mouth to speak, coughed up an explosion of blood that splashed down her chin and across her chest. She reached up as if trying to hold something back, but she didn't have the strength. She let her hand fall to her side. Her lips drew back in pain revealing bloody teeth, and then she seemed to collapse inward on herself as she died.

Tynan eased her head down, away from the wall so that she was lying flat on the floor. He pulled her blouse together so that her blood-covered breasts were hidden from sight.

"Shit!" he said.

Sterne appeared at his side. "Skipper, don't you think we should get out of here?"

"What about the guards outside?" he asked, getting to his feet.

"Arturo's boys said that the rest of them scrammed when the shooting started. Must have figured that it was all over up here and they had better get while the getting was good."

"Okay. Have someone make a stretcher for the girl and then you and Arturo sweep along the trail looking for an ambush. Take a couple of others, once you're through get back here and we'll all split."

Sterne looked down at Hamilton's body. Her skirt had hiked up, revealing her thighs. He crouched and adjusted her skirt so that it was covering her knees. "What about her?" asked Sterne as he stared at her body.

"Leave her with the rest of the terrorist bastards," said Tynan.

"Aye aye, sir," said Sterne. "I just thought that since she was an American we might want to do something for her. Get her out of here."

Tynan nodded. "Good thought. We'll take care of it." As Sterne disappeared through the door, Tynan took another look at Hamilton. He realized that he could have said something nicer to her as she died. Somehow it didn't seem right that the last thing she ever heard was someone accusing her of being a diseased whore.

13

Tynan watched as Arturo had the men make a stretcher for Juana Gutierrez from a blanket and two long poles. They laid it next to her and lifted her gently onto it. She didn't struggle or whine or whimper. She allowed them to do what they wanted to her.

That done, Tynan went into the back room. He ripped the sheet from the bed and took it into the front. Carefully he spread it over Hamilton's body. He looked at her face a last time. For an instant he had hated her because she had been opposed to everything that he believed in. And then, suddenly, he realized that she had been convinced she was right. She had sacrificed herself in a desperate attempt to recover something from the kidnapping. They couldn't force the generalissimo to resign because they would no longer hold his daughter, so she was going to make him suffer.

"I'm sorry about what I said," he told her. "No matter how misguided your motives, at least you believed enough to die for your cause."

He let the sheet fall back, covering her face. He stood up and moved to the door. He saw Sterne sprinting up the path.

"Skipper, I think they're coming back."

Tynan looked at him questioningly.

"Arturo is spreading the men out in the woods. We make it twenty, twenty-five guys. Couldn't make out the weapons, but I think they're carrying AKs. Nothing heavier."

Tynan rubbed his face with one hand quickly. "Okay, get the girl into the back room, on the floor under the mattress, and protect her as best you can." He pointed to Boone. "Kick the table over and push it up against the wall there. You two guys, barricade that area under the window there."

Tynan turned. "Sterne, I want you to stay in the back room with the girl. Keep a watch out the window."

"Aye aye, Skipper."

Tynan moved to the doorway and looked out. "Kill the lights," he said. Outside he could see nothing moving. He ducked back and said, "Remember, we have people out there too. Be sure of your targets before shooting."

Again he looked out and thought that he saw a shape moving among the trees two hundred yards away. He kept his eyes on it and got down to his belly. He rested his chin on the stock of his M-16 as the Army instructor in a night firing course had taught him and pulled the trigger once. Even with the flash suppressor a tongue of flame shot from the end of the rifle, momentarily blinding him. He didn't know whether he hit his target or not. There was no answering fire.

Off to the left, in the woods where he had hidden earlier, Tynan heard a burst of automatic weapons fire. It sounded like an M-16 and it was answered by two AK-47s. Tynan had seen no muzzle flashes.

Suddenly, almost directly in front of him, not more than fifty, sixty yards away, shapes loomed out of the dark. One of them seemed to lean back, one arm outstretched in front as if aiming, the other cocked back, near the right ear. The body propelled itself forward.

"Grenade!" yelled Tynan as he rolled to the left so that he was behind the wall, away from the door.

The men around him dropped to the floor, covering their heads with their arms. Outside, there was a tiny thud as the grenade landed on the ground and rolled, exploding far short of the farmhouse, its shrapnel losing its sting before it could reach the defenders.

Tynan rolled back and let a five-shot burst fly, watching the single tracer as it looped outward, hit something solid, and bounced high into the air, spinning end over end. He glanced to the right where he heard sustained firing, caught a couple of the muzzle flashes, but was sure that it was his and Arturo's men shooting at the shadows and shapes.

At that moment, another grenade hit the ground near him, rolling through the door. Tynan snatched at it, found it, and threw it back, dropping flat as he yelled, "Grenade!"

It exploded in the air overhead, raining shrapnel over a thirty-meter area, but there was no one near it.

Tynan flipped his selector to full auto and fired three quick bursts, emptying his weapon. He rolled to his left side as he ejected the empty magazine and replaced it with a fresh one. As he glanced out the door, he saw three shapes running left to right, out of the trees, toward a depression on the other side of the cabin. He fired at them, a quick short burst, and then a longer one. He heard a scream of pain and saw two of the men go down, but the third made it to his objective, diving headlong into it.

All around the firing increased in intensity. The night sparkled with the muzzle flashes of the automatic weapons and rifles of both sides. The periodic explosions of hand grenades created fountains of sparks that momentarily lit everything like the strobe of a camera.

Tynan rolled to the other side of the door, looking out, toward the woods to the left. He could hear firing there and could see an occasional muzzle flash. Then, suddenly, a group of men were running straight at him. Tynan turned to fire and saw one of the men throw something that sailed through the door over his head, landing on the dirt floor somewhere behind him.

"Grenade!" he yelled. "Grenade!"

Just as all the men dropped, it exploded, the shrapnel riddling the walls around them, but most of it passed harmlessly over their heads. Some of it was absorbed by the chairs or the bench near the sink. Tynan felt something strike the heel of his boot. A sharp, quick rap as if he had been tapped on the foot by a baseball bat with little power behind it.

He looked out the door to see a group of men sprinting at him across the last of the open ground. Tynan raised the barrel of his rifle slightly and began shooting, firing short bursts. He saw a man fall, heard a second scream and then start limping, and then hit a third, driving him to the ground.

And then the men were fleeing, no longer shooting, but running, sprinting away from the cabin, dodging around the obstacles in their path, jumping over the bodies of their fallen comrades. One turned to shoot as if providing covering fire and was immediately cut down by several bursts from several automatic weapons.

Tynan got to his feet and fired a couple of shots into the night. He turned, leaned back against the rough wood of the wall and asked, "Anyone hurt?"

He heard a couple of the men respond that they were all right. Then he yelled at Sterne, "You both okay back there?"

"Fine, Skipper."

"Stay put for a minute. I think that's got it, but you can't tell with fanatics. They may try to rush us again."

Tynan turned back and looked out the door. He saw someone leave the woods and approach cautiously. As the man neared the door, he called out.

"I'm coming in."

"Come ahead, Arturo," said Tynan. "We've got you covered."

Arturo entered and crouched on the other side of the door, out of sight of those outside and nearly lost in the shadows inside. "They have left the area. Fled down the valley."

"You sure?"

"Yes. One of my men followed them for a short distance. They didn't stop running. Ten, fifteen of them, throwing away their guns, fleeing for their lives. I don't think they'll take up the terrorist mantle again soon."

Even in the dark Tynan could see a flash of white teeth. "Okay," he said. "Get some security out."

Arturo nodded and got to his feet. He glanced out the door and then sprinted into the trees.

"Lights. Turn on the lights," ordered Tynan, and then immediately regretted saying anything as the lights came on. He blinked rapidly and thought about visual purple and rods and cones and night vision.

Behind him, on the floor, he saw that the body of Hamilton had moved. The sheet covering her was riddled by shrapnel from the grenade that had exploded back there, and it explained why there had been no friendly casualties in the explosion.

Tynan smiled at her and said, "So, switched sides again and helped us." He moved to the sheet and looked under it. The shrapnel had shredded part of her skirt and riddled one of her legs, but there was no blood in the wounds, just torn flaps of skin. The grenade had mutilated her. He shook his head and thought about it. Somehow it didn't seem fair.

Sterne appeared in the doorway. "What's the plan of action, Skipper?"

"We're going to get out of here just as soon as I can arrange it."

"It's a long haul back to the cars."

Tynan nodded and got out his map, studying it. "I don't want to move down the road from here because we don't know who's going to be on the path. Seems to me that we could move one group back over the ridge and down to the roads there while another goes back to the vehicles."

"Why split up?" asked Sterne.

"Because Arturo and a couple of his men can make better time without us to slow them down. Besides, someone is going to have to carry the girl and that's going to slow us down even more. Makes sense to send someone for the cars."

Arturo reappeared then and said, "I've pulled my men back. Nobody was hurt in all that shooting."

"Good." He moved back to the upturned table and righted it before smoothing his map out on it. He explained how he wanted to withdraw from the cabin. Arturo nodded.

Boone came back in and collapsed into one of the chairs. "I have a tremendous headache," he said. "Absolutely, positively tremendous."

"We'll get you some aspirin in a couple of hours," said Tynan. He glanced back at Arturo. "You have any questions before we split?"

"No. I will take my men and leave now. Meet you at the rendezvous in a few hours."

It was a week after the shootout in the mountain cabin. Juana Gutierrez was back at home, under her father's care and protection and supposedly making a remarkable recovery. Suzy Hamilton's body had been retrieved from the cabin and shipped back to the United States for burial, but not to Paducah, Kentucky, because no one there knew who she was. Arturo was back at the embassy, in his tiny fourth-floor office, making reports to a variety of intelligence networks that still ignored most of what he reported.

Tynan, along with Sterne, Jones, and Boone, who had a miniature square of white cloth covering his bullet wound, sat in the ambassador's office in the embassy, waiting for him to finish his speech. The office was the most luxurious that Tynan had been in during the mission. It outclassed General McKibben's by a mile and a half. It seemed that it took up nearly the entire floor. It had a wall of windows that looked out on downtown Quito and had an unparalleled view of the mountains in the background. The floors were hardwood, covered with a variety of carpets, some of them undoubtedly woven in Ecuador. The furniture was the finest that money could buy. Fine dark woods worked by highly skilled craftsmen. Tynan wouldn't be surprised to learn that the ambassador's desk cost ten thousand dollars.

The ambassador had carefully read the entire report that Tynan had given him and then sat there for a moment, behind his castlelike desk, as if to digest the contents of the report. Finally he began to speak.

"I am not pleased," the ambassador said, folding his manicured hands on the green felt blotter of his mahogany desk. "I can't count the number of laws you have violated. You have smuggled people and weapons into Ecuador and killed people. You have employed locals to help in your massacre and then asked for us to pay them. Pay hired assassins. Mercenaries. You've done all this on a flimsy blank check issued by the State Department, but without anything at all in writing. I'm at a total loss for words here."

Tynan got to his feet. "Mr. Ambassador, I gave you the report as a courtesy. No one at my end even thought you should be told. They thought we should just sneak out of here like we came in. Quietly and undercover. I found a mole in your organization and have eliminated her. I have recovered the daughter of an ally and destroyed the hierarchy of a terrorist group, not to mention their support base and training camp. I have completed an assignment that should have been handled by the CIA if we felt the local population was incapable of the job. I never asked for it and in fact didn't want it. I have—"

The ambassador held up a hand. "Mr. Tynan, I am only telling you my feelings. I have spent my life in diplomacy and don't believe that resorting to violence here was all that necessary. However, I will grant that you have done your job with a minimum of attention from the various media, and the solution, while morally abhorrent, is nonetheless, satisfactory. At least it was satisfactory to the people in the State Department who requested your assistance.''

''Which means?'' asked Sterne, unable to restrain himself any longer.

''Simply that I will not forward an unsatisfactory report to your headquarters. I will, however, make a note of your names, and if you ever enter Ecuador again, I will find it necessary to report your activities to the local government and notify our government that you are considered as undesirable elements here in Ecuador.''

''Christ!'' exploded Sterne. ''I don't understand this at all. We did exactly what you people wanted and were unable to do yourselves with all your diplomatic bullshit, and you treat us like a mess the dog made.''

The ambassador gestured with his manicured hand. ''I am sorry if that is the impression you received. I only want to point out that diplomatic channels were being followed and progress was being made. I don't believe we needed you to rush in, guns blazing, shooting everyone and burning everything in sight.''

''And while your diplomatic channels were being followed,'' snapped Sterne, ''that girl was being tortured. A young, innocent girl being tortured, while you assholes talked to the fucking terrorists about—''

''*Sterne!*'' shouted Tynan. ''That will be enough. More than enough.''

Sterne glanced at him, his face a mask of anger, but said only, ''Aye aye, Skipper.''

The ambassador turned his attention back to Tynan. ''I realize that we travel in different circles, live in different worlds. I was merely indicating that we were having some success with our negotiations.''

"You can't negotiate with terrorists," said Tynan. "That only encourages them. What you do is shoot them as quickly as you can. And when they take hostages to demand that other terrorists be freed, you end the situation quickly and execute those that the terrorists demanded. You eliminate the problem. You make terrorism a deadly game for the terrorists. If they try something, they must know they are going to die.''

"That won't stop the fanatic," said the ambassador. "The fanatic won't be swayed by threats of death.''

"No, but it will stop the Sunday enthusiast. If they know they're going to die, they're going to think twice about it. Now they know that they're probably going to live and if captured, sentenced to prison, because, God forbid, we don't want to kill the little darlings.''

"You may be right, Mr. Tynan," the ambassador agreed reluctantly, "you may be right, but diplomacy has its place in this arena too.''

Tynan looked at the floor and rubbed his head. This was not what he had expected. A veiled ass-chewing and a discussion on the politics of terror. He had hoped that someone would be sufficiently impressed with the activities of the last few days to give them a few words of praise. They had done an impossible job, done it with no friendly casualties, and all the ambassador would say was that he wouldn't write a negative report if Tynan and his men got out of the country as quickly as was humanly possible.

"I believe," said Tynan, "that we'll just leave now. Thank you for providing the passports that Mr.

Sterne and Mr. Boone needed. Passports with the proper entry stamps and visas attached.''

The ambassador got to his feet. "It was the least I could do,'' he said.

They left the ambassador's office. As they waited for the elevator, ignoring the stairs to the left, Boone asked, "Now what?''

"I guess,'' answered Tynan, "that since no one has issued any new orders, or amended our old ones, that we return to the survival school in Panama.''

Sterne groaned. "Jesus. I would think that we just proved that we didn't need to go to any damned survival school. We were resourceful, we hiked through the mountains, and we succeeded at our mission.''

"But we didn't get to eat any chicken-tasting snakes,'' said Jones, grinning.

The elevator arrived and opened. They all entered and Tynan pushed the button for the ground floor. As the doors shut, he said, "A good, successful mission. I agree. But since our orders call for us to spend a month in Panama and there is still a week left on those orders, we'll have to go back to Panama. Maybe General McKibben can be convinced that we should practice survival on the base rather than in the jungle.''

"That's not much of a reward for a job well done,'' said Boone.

"No,'' said Tynan. "It's not much of a reward, but then, that's all there is.''